13,99

Alice in Thunderland

MAEVE KELLY

Attic Press
DUBLIN

First published in Ireland in 1993 by
Attic Press
4 Upper Mount Street
Dublin 2

British Library Cataloguing in Publication Data
Kelly, Maeve
Alice in Thunderland
I. Title
823.914
ISBN 1 85594 081 7

Cover Design: Trina Mahon
Illustrations: Trina Mahon
Origination: Verbatim Typesetting and Design
Printing: Guernsey Press Co Ltd

This book is published with the assistance of The Arts Council/An Chomhairle Ealaíon.

Dedication

To the memory of Una and Ellen,
a lovely daughter and a wonderful mother
who have gone before me.

About the Author

Maeve Kelly is the author of two collections of short stories, *A Life of Her Own* and *Orange Horses*, two novels, *Necessary Treasons* and *Florrie's Girls* and a collection of poetry, *Resolution*. She lives outside Limerick.

Chapter One

Alice discovered Thunderland by chance. She had been fishing for sprackerels off the shore of Harmony Isle when she fell asleep. While she was asleep, one of those freak currents that occasionally sweeps past islands in the northern hemisphere brought her out to the middle of the ocean. For ten days and nights she drifted. She had had the foresight to bring her normal life-support supplies in her bag, something that all Harmonisers were trained to do from an early age. She had several sprackerels which she salted each day, using the brine from the sea. Her desalinating tablets provided her with ample if unpalatable water, and her protective cream prevented the worst effects of exposure. Nonetheless, in spite of all these aids to survival, she was delighted when, after ten days of nothing but sea and sky, she sighted land at last.

As soon as she spotted it she realised it must be Thunderland. There were the inevitable black clouds and crackling noises. But no lightning. In Harmony they occasionally had storms which were so ferocious that everyone went into hiding until they were over. They were electric storms, and whilst anyone who ventured out into the open was certain to be killed, they were of great benefit to the economy of the country since they charged the receivers from which most of their energy came. In Thunderland there were great flurries of noise and lots of gloom.

Thunderland was something of a joke in Harmony Isle, although many of the older sisters had solemn faces when they spoke of it and said one could never be sure of memblies and femblies, the inhabitants of Thunderland, and that the less intercourse there was with them the better. The magnetic field developed by the Harmonisers to keep out invaders had so far protected them from unwelcome visitors. Alice thought her elders were over-cautious, but she recognised that caution was a side-kick of wisdom, which was acquired only after years of experience and intelligent observation.

However, it was quite exciting to be able to view Thunderland at first hand. She steered her boat directly towards the safest landing place and with a feeling of awe set foot for the first time in the country of the memblies and femblies. She looped her survival bag around her shoulders and set off to explore.

'I would just love a drink of fresh spring water,' Alice said to herself, 'but there doesn't seem to be any around.' Just then a huge black cloud moved and let down its load of water directly over her head. She quickly made a little receptacle of leaves and held the dish against the nearest tree, down which the water was already cascading.

'Hey there,' a voice from the top of the tree said peremptorily. 'Have you got your card? You must first show your green card and then your orange card before you are allowed to—Atch—Atch—oo.'

'To atchoo?' Alice asked in bewilderment. 'What is that?'

'Stupid fem,' the voice muttered. 'Can't you see I'm allergic to fems. Clear off before I have you arrested for leaning on a mem preserve.

Alice backed away and looked up and down to find the source of this strange voice. She was about to conclude that she had imagined the conversation when a young creature leaped down from the tree and said,

'Card please?'

'I've already told you I haven't got one.'

'You said no such thing.'

'I told you by thought. Didn't you pick it up?'

'Pick it up? Pick up thought. What next! If you have no card there is an on-the-spot fine. No beer, ale, porter or whisky with your breakfast on Sunday, that's the penalty.'

'I don't drink any of that.'

'No football, boxing, cock-fighting, badger-baiting.'

'I don't... '

No mud-tussling.'

'I don't...'

'Don't say don't. Fems are not allowed to say "won't" or "don't".' And he marched off in a rage, his head high and his arms swinging.

'Don't mind him, my dear,' a voice from behind her said. 'You're a stranger here, I assume. How did you come?'

'I came here by boat. A freak current seemed to carry...'

But he wasn't listening.

'I am the Bearded One,' he said proudly. 'I am the Tall One.' He had six sprigs of hair on his chin and he just about reached to her shoulder.

He walked around her, examining her critically. 'What is your name? You're big for your age. We can't have that. Rule 745 of the constitution has something to say on the proper height for fems.' He flicked hurriedly through the pages of a book he pulled out of his tunic pocket.

'My name is...' Alice began.

'Speak when you're spoken to. Fems corner only. Fem topics, hours 8–12, 4–6 pm, evening, post midday. Come with me.'

'Curiouser and curiouser,' Alice thought. 'Where will this all lead? It will be interesting to find out.'

'It might not be as interesting as you think,' a voice to her left said. With that, the Bearded One shrieked and rushed at the voice.

'If I catch you around my property I'll beat your head off.'

'Property! Property!' Alice said indignantly. 'I like that.'

'So you should,' the other voice said in between gasps as he and the Bearded One thumped each other with their sticks. 'I am Picky Brains. I especially like—thump, thump, gasp, gasp—picking fem brains and this gubu hates it. Ow!'

'That's only telepathy. Not very original.'

'It's not telepathy. It's brain-picking. You twilic. Brain-picking. Ow, Son of Zebob. Sunshine spreader. Take that.'

The Bearded One was laid low.

'That was quick,' Alice said, 'and very unnecessary. You're twice his size. You're as big as I am.'

'I'm twice your size.' The creature drew himself up to his full height. He was an elasticised person, able to stretch himself by expanding all his muscles. 'Twice as high and twice as handsome.' To Alice's amazement he threw himself on the ground and began to lever himself up on his arms and legs, keeping his body rigid while he counted between grunts. Then he gathered himself together and leaped to his feet, beat his chest and said, 'Thirty, thirty. Better and better. Have you done yours? You should be in the fems' corner doing yours. It's exercise time.'

'Why do you have exercise time?' Alice asked. 'Don't you work?'

'Work? You mean work-outs?'

'Well…in and out. We work inside and outside in Harmony Isle.'

'Inside and outside,' the creature said. 'Division of labour. We have progressed beyond that. We have machines.'

'Oh, we had machines a long time ago,' Alice said, 'but we overcame them. They are all banished now. We run our own lives now. We use imagination and cooperation.'

'Who wants to run a life? Run a race, a supermarket, run a draw for the biggest prize. They are runs. You're very talkative for a fem. Where did you learn? Here they just chatter. And only at preordained times. They have a kind of infantile language they use for communication.'

'You talk,' Alice said.

'I'm a membly. You're only a fembly. Femblies communicate by sign language outside of chatter-time.'

'You must be wrong,' Alice said.

He turned black with rage and stretched to his full elasticated height. 'Wrong!' he screamed and a great peal of thunder echoed his rage. The sky grew dark. Rain poured down, drenching both of them. 'You can be imprisoned for that. Stupid fem. You'll get me into trouble for even talking to you.' He seemed to turn into a snake and slithered off behind a rock.

Alice had taken shelter under an overhanging stone and was sitting reflecting on the strange behaviour of the creatures she had met when she heard a sound. Around the nearest bush there appeared six memblies dragging three poles between them. They stopped and looked around furtively. 'We'll put them up here,' one who appeared to be the leader said. 'If anyone sees us doing it without a machine, it will be no pints on Sunday.'

'There are no pole machines yet.'

'You should have invented one.'

'Oh I hadn't the paper to draw the diagram. I hadn't the list of equipment. I hadn't the application for the feasibility study. I hadn't the projected profits. I've been too busy.'

'Well, I just hope its OK.'

'Let me help,' Alice said, coming out of her shelter.

'My God, it's a fembly,' the leader said.

One came forward and poked a finger at her. 'It speaks of its own accord.'

Alice reacted by kicking his hand down and throwing him on the ground. The five memblies pulled back in amazement.

'How did she do that?'

'Rush her,' one said. 'If we all rush together we'll get her.' Alice was angry.

'I don't wish to be poked,' she said. From her pocket she pulled her flexible whip and began to flick it at their feet. They danced back. 'I can slice your heads off with this,' Alice warned, 'if I consider myself provoked.'

'A nasty piece of goods,' they said to each other. 'She must have escaped from the training centre.

'Ignore her. She's not worth it. Let's get on with the shrine.'

'Have a pint first?'

They sat in a circle and produced bottles from their inside pockets.

'We haven't had a muse for ages,' one said. 'She can be our muse.'

They then widened the circle and Alice allowed herself to be within its perimeter. She kept a tight hold of her whip because she knew she was in great danger. But she felt the information gleaned from this unfamiliar behaviour would add to her understanding. The risk was calculable and therefore worth it.

The six, having consumed their pints, took it in turns to drone in sad monotonous voices. As each finished, the others nodded wisely, applauded and made comments. Every now and again one speaker would turn his back. When that happened the others nudged each other and winked and made rude faces, indicating to Alice that his work was very bad. She found their behaviour remarkable for its inconsistency and was intent on studying them when one of the group stood up and said solemnly, 'I remember.' The others joined in a solemn chant

I remember Brendan of the Beehives and the great pints.
I remember Paddy the Cadaverous and the great belly aches.
I remember Jimín Seoighe and the great blooming bus journey.
I remember Liam and all his works and pomps.
I remember Flannel and the wide and woolly underpants.
Tee hee hee Tee hee hee Let us here laugh.
I remember Bracket the sad and lonely one.
Oh the emptiness.
Oh
Flat.
Without meaning.
Life.
Death.
Pain.
Emptiness.
Long road to nowhere.

Each word was uttered in a deep portentous voice.

'It must be a different language,' thought Alice. 'Such words are fairly significant but quite common. People here seem to believe the ordinary is miraculous. I wonder if they also believe the miraculous to be ordinary. Perhaps they do not experience as we experience and therefore exaggerate everything. I think I will test one for pain.'

With that she tentatively flicked her whip, catching the small dark hairy one who happened to be nearest her. He let out a great roar and clutched his leg in amazement.

'She hit me. That fuzzing fem hit me. I'll break every bone in her body.'

'Watch that whip,' his companions advised him, with some wisdom, Alice had to admit.

'I must warn you,' she said, 'I am champion whip-cracker in my own land. I apologise if I hurt you. I thought perhaps you mightn't feel pain as we do?'

'What did she say?'

They glared at her and at each other. 'We can't have this. We'll have to do something with this creature.'

'I know what I'd like to do with her,' one said, and they all began to laugh in a peculiar way. It was as if they had a secret signal, for a strange glitter came into their eyes and they began to make little dancing steps with hands outstretched as if they hoped to prevent her escape. Suddenly their movements became very fast and one actually managed to pull at the sleeve of her coat. It tore.

Alice said, 'Well that it,' and she cast the whip around the group so that it coiled in a wide arc. It enclosed them in its whistling circle, pulling them to the ground. Gasping and cursing, they struggled on top of each other.

'Nicely parcelled,' she said.

'It's not fair,' they grumbled. 'You've got a weapon. We have none.' Alice laughed heartily, thinking the remark was a joke. When she realised that they weren't laughing she sighed in disappointment, uncoiled her whip and left them arguing with one another about who was to blame for their downfall.

Chapter Two

At the end of her first day in Thunderland Alice felt exhausted. She had met the strangest creatures imaginable. Her effort to understand them was beginning to produce a dangerous lethargy which she had never before experienced but which, she knew from her training manual, had to be resisted.

Her lethargy was in strong contrast to the excitement and energy she seemed to produce in those she met—who were, of course, all memblies. She had not met one single fembly. She might have believed they did not exist were it not for the fact that they were so frequently mentioned in the memblies' conversations. References were always disparaging, the mildest being a phrase frequently repeated, 'Oh, femblies,' accompanied by a raucous laugh or a peculiar curling of the lip which she recognised as conveying distaste or contempt.

There were other customs which she was not yet able to identify and her inability to decode them added to her weariness. She tried the various reasoning methods she had been taught in Harmony Isle, beginning with 'cool assessment', but the memblies talked so loudly and with such strength of belief that it was impossible to escape their verbal assaults. Their words had the force of weapons. They seemed to surround her with their extraordinary logic and she began to feel not only tired but hemmed-in.

It was time for seclusion, she decided. She found a convenient nook under a bush and curled herself into a little ball, turning herself into herself to recharge her interior strength while resting. She shut eye and deafed ear, so enclosing herself in her capsule of being that restoration might be quickly achieved. However, as a wise precaution, so that she might not be totally unaware, (a dangerous state in this Thunderland), she left on her extra-sensory perceptions.

Fifteen minutes later they registered feeling. She woke up, completely refreshed and relaxed, and uncurled herself from self to take note of her perception. Somewhere in the vicinity something was happening. The vibrations were remarkable. She resumed seeing and hearing and wound her way through a curving path (the first curve she had come across) to their source.

Two creatures were sitting by a stream, staring into the water. One was definitely a membly; she could tell by the set of the head on the neck and by the shape of its shoulders. They weren't square exactly, but they had a kind of bluntness about them, an assertion of something or other. It didn't matter to Alice what they were asserting. It just struck her as odd that they did. The other creature was definitely not a membly. Alice had met enough of them to be certain. This creature had a different set of head. Her body coordination was subtler and more supple. Her voice, when she spoke, had something of the timbre of Alice's and it was this voice which had activated her vibrations. There was no doubt in Alice's mind. This creature must be the missing fembly. At long last she was going to meet the female variety. They must be very scarce, Alice thought. She had met sixty-three memblies and this was the first fembly. Sixty-three to one was long odds. No cat race would be worth an entry in Harmony Isle if the odds were so high. They must have a scarcity value. She calculated the odds versus scarcity equation, using the formula for dissimilar forces and the answer was farce. Oh dearie me, thought Alice and then was struck by the voice.

It appeared to be crying.

'I can't stand any more,' the voice was saying, 'I just can't stand it...'

'You're always saying that,' the membly replied. 'I don't know what's wrong with you. You have everything.

'I have nothing. Nothing. I am nothing,' the fembley's voice anguished. 'I wish I were dead.'

Alice clapped her hands to her ears. The pain of this remark made her reel.

'Oh forgive forgive,' she cried in response. 'Forgive. Forgive.' Her pain eased. She rushed towards the couple, intending to help the membly restore the life-wish to his partner. But to her astonishment he calmly reached for a green bag lying on the grass, from which he drew out some wriggling worms. He then attached them to a long line on a stick.

The fembly stood up and moved away from him. The death-wish was heavy in her heart. It beat and whined and snarled and moaned. Alice began the forgive chant but nothing could keep the pain from taking over. She rushed out in front of the creature crying, 'Stop, stop.'

The death-wish faded.

'It gave me a headache. Why did you do it?' Alice asked the fembly

'I didn't do anything. What business is it of yours? I was having a private conversation. It is not civil to eavesdrop.'

'A private conversation?' Alice tried to work out what this might be.

'What did Eve drop?' she asked helpfully.

'Very funny, I don't think,' the girl sneered, 'Eve dropped her knickers, of course. It's always the same.'

'Did she lose the knickers?' Alice asked. 'Did she want them badly? Did she miss them? Is that why you made the death-wish?'

'You're a crazy person,' the fembly said, backing away.

Alice didn't want her to go. If she couldn't understand this creature who was surely something like herself, judging from the vibrations, how would she ever be able to understand the others? The whole adventure was becoming almost too risky. If she was attacked by any more confusion then she might become too weak to make her way back. She made a quick assessment of her remaining resources. With sufficient retreat time for self-confirmation she should be able to manage. In any case, her virtue of insatiable curiosity had to be nourished and used.

In Harmony Isle her gift had produced many useful devices which had given everyone much happiness. Even here in this danger country she might learn and achieve.

'I felt your death-wish,' she said carefully, choosing the words delicately. 'I felt for you.'

With these words the fembly suddenly began to make the most horrible noise Alice had ever heard. Water flowed in torrents from her eyes, spilling down her cheeks and on to the ground. A little rivulet formed at Alice's feet and she felt herself sinking, sinking down. She closed her eyes and concentrated. If it be for good, let me go down. If I learn and achieve, let me go down. She felt the earth subside under her and just as she went spinning down, down into another territory the fembly clasped her arms around her, still letting the water gush from her eyes, but with the dreadful sound now silenced.

Alice opened her eyes. Much to her relief the fembly had stopped watering but she still clung to Alice.

'My golly,' she said, 'I've heard of this place but I never thought I would find myself in it. How did you manage it? You're a right weirdo. What will the lirgs say when I tell them? They'll never believe it. They certainly won't believe it.' She began to hum to herself, a pleasant little tune which Alice picked up and sang with pleasure.

'What place is it?' she asked, but without waiting for an answer and shaking herself free of the fembly's grip so that she could investigate.

'It's the funnery,' the fembly said. 'The only funnery in the whole of Thunderland. This is where all the laughing and singing and making and doing goes on. The funns were banished years ago because they were too powerful and too optimistic. They were for change and they used to say treasonable things like...' she paused and put her hand to her forehead. 'I've forgotten. I used to know. My grandmother taught me a few of the lines but they were all wiped out by relearning and of course by ignoring. Ignoring and silence are very important parts of femblies' education.'

Alice was sure she had picked up a dodo. A dumb-dumb. This creature was even worse than the memblies. She glanced cautiously at her to see if her brains were showing.

'Have you brains?' Alice asked politely.

The fembly became very agitated.

'You mustn't say that. Someone might hear. Oh, I forgot. It's safe here. I used to have more brains but some of them turned into feathers. Look.'

Sure enough a little tuft of feathers showed through

her hair.

'How did you get those?' Alice asked with interest.

'It took a long time. I had to read the prescribed texts and never ask the questions I wanted to ask. I had to learn not to do the things I thought were useful, or to think the things I thought were important. That was very hard. I had to stifle imagination and turn down feeling. Femblies' feelings are too strong, you know. Every now and again they take over and they gush out in torrents. That's what happened a while ago.'

'Well,' Alice said. 'then it was your feelings that brought us here. It's a good trick. I must learn it. It's practically an achievement,' she added kindly, not wishing to sound begrudging.

'I remember, I remember,' the fembly cried aloud. 'I remember grandmother's sayings. Beware of the dirty tricks brigade. Always look a gift horse twenty times. Never sign on the dotted line. Never say I do. Always ask why. Worry about a persecution complex when the persecutor is dead. Grow a wisteria for the doctor's hysteria. A woman wears an apron to cook a banquet. A man wears a crown to boil a haddock.'

She would have continued but Alice's attention had been taken by a great construction looming out of the dark undergrowth in front of them. It was like an enormous yellow drum. On its round face a huge sunflower was painted and Alice then noticed that the sides of the clearing where they had landed were lined with sunflowers, apparently growing upside down. Their stalks trailed upwards towards the sky, their heads rested on the ground below them, releasing a gentle yellow light.

The centre of the sunflower on the building was a

huge smiling face. The petals consisted of a circle of arms waving and gesticulating. As Alice and the fembly approached, the face spoke. It sounded like chiming bells.

'Welcomy, welcomy. Come in, well and truly dearest friends. Open your hearts and your minds, my treasures, my pets. My dotey ones. Oh, pulse of my hearts and brightness of brightness. Enter the place of happiness. Pray be seated if you will, or pray stand if you will not. Happily you may remember and happily you may forget. Whatever is mine is yours, whatever is yours is anyone's. Please enter on the sixth note. Thanking you, signing off, your best friend and delight of your life, my love, my dove, my beautiful one. Afem.'

Alice was busily engaged in translating this effusive welcome when the sixth bell chimed, the mouth which had been uttering the words turned into an elaborate doorway, a silver-coloured drawbridge was lowered and two beautiful long-haired, silver-eyed, pink-furred cats stepped out of the sunflower, curtsying as they came to Alice and the fembly.

'Your pleasure is our pleasure,' they sang in unison, perfectly in tune. 'Follow us to the gathering of the funns. You are just in time to hear the first debate. We have been awaiting you.'

Oh, I feel sick,' the fembly groaned.

'Breathe deeply, count to ten, think of your grandmother,' Alice instructed.

They followed the pink cats along the silver roadway through the sunflower door-mouth and into the most splendid of palaces. As they entered they had to duck all the waving petal arms whose hands were catching at Alice's hair, the fingers getting entangled and pulling tufts of it out. Alice was not too pleased at this. She frowned a little.

Instantly a great bell boomed throughout the building. Lights flashed purple, yellow, orange, green, blue, spotted, striped in an incredible combination of colours. The cats leaped and hissed and stared at Alice, arching their backs, their silvery eyes gleaming.

The fembly clung to Alice's arm. In front of them, great purple velvet curtains swished to one side, revealing rows of creatures with their heads turned and their hundreds of laughing eyes directed straight at Alice. One of them stood up. She was about Alice's own height. Her hair was silky and striped with pink and yellow bars. It hung over her shoulders. She was wearing coloured balloons. As she moved they continually burst and she continually laughed, blew up another and attached it wherever she pleased.

'You frowned,' she said sweetly. 'You set our alarms off. Did you have a bad thought, you nasty thing?'

Alice was surprised to find herself amused by her question and not in the least wearied because she did not understand. The creature was so merry and the colours so enchanting that she felt a cloudy haze envelop her thought. Just in time she switched on her protection from exaggerated impulses and the cloud shifted.

The creature who had addressed her appeared to be the head of the funnery. She twiddled her fingers and all the funns rose up and sang, 'Pale, poley, pea, pother of Percy, pale'. They burst out laughing, leaped out of their seats and began to dance extravagantly, throwing their legs and arms around, shaking their heads, while the room filled with the sound of music from hundreds of instruments.

The fembly was overcome with joy and rushed to join them, singing in a strange high voice in an unfamiliar language. Alice began to laugh and the more she laughed the louder grew the singing. Her head began to swim with the noise. Her own laughter made her sick.

'Stop,' she cried, 'you foolish creatures. Show me what you can make or do.'

As if she had turned a switch, everything stopped. At a signal from the head funn, all the funns filed past her towards another room. The fembly was lost in the crowd. She seemed to have been swallowed up. Alice followed the crowd. Their previously rainbow-coloured clothes were being changed before her eyes into peculiar dark-grey body and leg covers. They wore white tops under these grey coverings and around their necks were dark strips of cloth, hidden under the collars, but appearing as a narrow line on the top. Alice wondered if they could be choked by these ties, if the blood supply to their brains might not be impeded, but she was interested in seeing how these, the first of the femblies she had met in Thunderland, occupied their time usefully. They would surely be better than the word-worshipping memblies she had met earlier and whom she had been obliged to whip into line when they tried to take advantage of her.

She was last to enter the next room, apart from the two pink cats who trailed behind her, obviously keeping their silver eyes on her. All the funns were seated in rows of benches and had already begun working on an enormous, intricately worked lace cloth. It seemed to Alice that there were acres and acres of this beautiful material. The funns had their heads bent and their nimble fingers moved quickly through the delicate patterns. The head funn sat at a table and held up a picture of a bearded membly who had a sunflower over his head, but was unmistakably a membly nonetheless.

'Remember,' the head funn said, 'My sisters, my dears. Your work is for the good of your soles so that your feet may dance nimbly and will do honour at the same time to our dear Rescuer. Let us give thanks. Let us play. But not just yet.'

'What are they making?' Alice asked, 'and who is the Rescuer?'

'The rescuer is the chief of all time and place and space and everything and nothing. The funns make trimmings for the memblies who guard his presence.'

'But I thought you said the memblies had banished the femblies,' Alice said, feeling confused. 'And isn't the Rescuer a membly? And couldn't the funns make a sail instead of this trimming so that they could get away from this terrible place?'

'It's not a terrible place,' the fembly said. 'It's full of love and sunshine.'

'They're only sunflowers,' Alice said. 'It's all artificial. I don't think much of it. I prefer proper sunshine. And when is the debate?'

'I'm going to water again,' the fembly gasped. 'You're ruining everything. I can feel a watering coming on.'

'I'll get you a bucket,' Alice said helpfully. But it was too late. The fembly had already begun. Waterfalls spilled from her eyes. In seconds the ground was a marsh. In minutes it was a lake. All the benches were turned upside down and the funns sat in them, paddling merrily with their hands. The head funn called out, 'In this time of crisis, let us begin our great debate.'

Alice managed to procure a small table for herself and pulled the fembly and the pink cats up to share it with her.

'I'd like to join in,' she called.

But the head funn had paddled away rapidly from her, shouting, 'Haven't you done enough damage? Go back where you came from. We can do without your sort here. Blow-in. Runner.'

Alice sighed heavily. They had gone through the now soggy velvet curtains and were being swept along towards the sunflower-mouth exit. What would await them outside? She was filled with even more insatiable curiosity. There were more adventures in store.

Chapter Three

Alice and the fembly reached the sunflower mouth just as the petals were closing inwards. 'Hurry, hurry,' gasped the fembly. 'If the flower closes on us we will never get out. We will be stuck here in the funnery for ever and ever.'

A fate to be avoided, Alice realised, grasping the fembly by the hair and swimming strongly towards the exit. Behind them the funns called, 'Wait, wait, dear sisters. Wait for our reunion. We will have a lovely get-together if you only wait.'

'They want to eat us,' the fembly gurgled through mouthfuls of water. 'I just know they want to eat us. They will eat us up and spit us out when they have finished.'

Alice was too busy swimming to reply. She had to push her away very strongly through the sunflower petals, which were sticky and clinging and heavily scented. In fact, the perfume was so strong it made Alice almost sleepy and when she looked down at the fembly she realised her new friend was indeed fast asleep.

'An interesting attempt at control,' Alice mused. Then they were out through the opening and into the undergrowth and suddenly her feet touched the ground. In the distance she saw a chink of blue light which she realised was the entrance to the tunnel down which they had tumbled. The fembly was by now snoring her head off, so Alice tucked her under her arm and made for the opening. Rocks, rubble and clay were piled up in an irregular pyramid and Alice clawed her way up it. About twenty feet separated her from the chink of blue light.

She uncoiled her whip from around her waist and whirled it around her head, carefully aiming at the exit. In a single throw the end of the whip was hooked into the earth above and she swung herself and her friend up its length and out into the open again.

The fembly woke up just as they flopped onto the ground.

'Wha'...wha' happened?' she asked. She didn't wait for an answer but proceeded with the next question. 'Did we miss the happening?'

'I don't know about that,' Alice said. 'But we missed being caught in the sunflower palace with the funns. A pretty difficult place to escape from, by the look of it.'

'It is, it is,' the fembly agreed. 'You have to get a pupil dissipation. And you might never get it. You have to apply in hectiplate and wait for a millennium of years which may or may not come. But you might like it there. Some people do.'

'You told me the funns were banished years ago because they were too powerful. You also said that all the singing and laughing and making and doing goes on there. Why would anyone want to stay in a place of banishment? I do not think I would like to be banished,' said Alice. 'And I don't think I would like to have to sing and laugh and make and do. I might like to think. I might like to cry. I might like to be sad.'

'You are not allowed to be sad,' the fembly said miserably. 'When femblies are sad we cry too much and we make enormous rivers. We create confusion, you know. When there's trouble, *sachet la fembly.*'

'What does that mean?' Alice asked with interest.

'I don't know,' the fembly said. 'How would I know? I'm just told and I believe what I am told. Faith is the thing. We must have faith.'

'Faith in what?' Alice asked for the sake of politeness, although she was beginning to find the conversation a little dull. She was a strange creature, this fembly, and yet it was hard not to like her. She had an amusing turn of phrase, thought Alice.

'Just faith. We'd better watch it. We are beginning to ask too many questions. I think I asked two questions a while ago. That could be my quota.' She began to count nervously on her fingers.

Fancy having a quota of questions, thought Alice. There were many irritating aspects to this Thunderland and she was beginning to wish she had never drifted on to its shore. The very first opportunity she got she would leave it. She looked down at the fembly trotting along beside her and wondered what would happen to her when she left her.

'Are you going to meet the membly you left fishing?'

'Oh no,' replied the fembly. 'He'll have found a new fembly for himself. Someone prettier and more glamorous than me. I was only a trial. I was his practice. I am always the practice.'

'What did you practise?' asked Alice.

'The usual things,' the fembly said. 'Slaving and choring and hearing and hooring.'

'It sounds disgusting,' Alice said.

'You get used to it,' the fembly replied philosophically. 'It's bad in the beginning because everything is all mixed up and you don't know which thing you are supposed to be doing. Sometimes you do the hooring and then you discover you should have been doing the choring and sometimes you do the hearing and then you realise you should have been doing the slaving. But after a while you begin to get the hang of it. The trouble is that when you're a practice you've just managed to understand the membly you've got when you're finished with him and you have to go to another one. Memblies use up a lot of femblies.'

'And were you always a practice or did you become one?'

'I became one of course.' The fembly seemed annoyed by Alice's question. 'You think I always looked like this? I was once pretty, you know.'

'I think you're pretty now,' Alice said politely. She had no idea what pretty meant, but she could see that it was important to the fembly.

'It doesn't matter if *you* think I am pretty,' the fembly said rudely. 'It's what the others think that matters.'

'The memblies?'

'Yes and no. They make some of the prettiness rules. But it is the *others* who make most rules. I can't explain it, and if you keep asking any more questions someone is bound to pick them up on the wavelengths and you will be tied to a stake and burned and you wouldn't like that, I can tell you.'

Alice burst out laughing. 'I'd like to see them try,' she said. 'Tie me to a stake! Burn me! What a joke.'

She was sorry she laughed because the fembly clapped her little hands to her pointy little ears and began to rock to and fro.

'Hale and rainbow, all hale and stones, pallyoola, afem, afem, so be it,' she chanted, and began to bob up and down, tipping her knee to the ground and then bowing her forehead until it touched the ground.

'You want to be careful,' Alice said. 'That is muddy.'

'She knoweth not what she sayeth,' the fembly cried.

'She knoweth not what she doeth.'

'I certainly do know what I sayeth and I certainly do know what I doeth,' Alice protested. But the poor fembly had such a look of anguish on her face and she was so busy contorting herself into the oddest positions that Alice knew she was truly upset. It occurred to Alice then that she had shut off all her own insights and instincts since she had come to this strange place and that she was beginning to lose the powers of understanding and of feeling.

'I am very sorry,' she said. 'I am very, very sorry. I apologise.'

'Oh, thank goodness.' The fembly straightened up. 'I thought you would never say it. You're some dumb broad, believe me.'

'I believe you,' Alice said sincerely. To her amazement the fembly smiled, a funny lopsided quiver of a smile but still a smile.

They had come to a crossroads of a sort.

'This is the Hand,' the fembly said. 'The thumb is the short road to Wordy, which is where all the fine talkers live. You need a pass for it and I don't have one. The forefinger goes to the Safe Confinement, the middle finger goes to the Boxing Match, the fourth finger—'

'I would like to see the Boxing Match,' Alice interrupted, her enthusiasm getting the better of her politeness. 'Do they box matches or match boxes?'

'You get weirder by the minute,' said the fembly. 'I have a feeling you won't like this.' The moment she said the words she clapped her hand over her mouth in horror and then to Alice's amazement she pulled her oddly shaped skirt over her face and began to rock to and fro. At the same time a siren screeched around them and a loud voice began to hector and command.

'Who is it that cometh over the mountain? Who is it that hath a feeling? Who is it that useth the word 'like'? Likes and dislikes, feelings and emotions. The fembly diseases have almost been conquered, the virus of feeling almost destroyed. Who would run the risk of their revival? Speak up. Identify yourself. Confess your sin and do penance.'

'I confess to all right and wrong. I confess to blather, Jung and holy fraud,' the fembly gabbled, frantically turning around in circles as she did so, 'that I have sinned impedingly, and withered the power of seed. My own fault, my own fault, my own fault. I'm to blame I'm to blame I'm to blame. I did it I did it I did it. I said it I said it I said it. *Sachet la fembly, sachet la fembly.*'

Alice looked everywhere for the source of the voice and just as the fembly had finished her frantic gyrations she noticed a familiar object on top of a nearby tree. Pulling out her whip, she flicked it in that direction. There was a splutter of blue and the object came tumbling down. It crackled for a few seconds and then went dead.

'A primitive piece of equipment,' Alice remarked, examining it. 'A microphone picks up the vibration—it's probably tuned to particular words—and then the loud-speaker broadcasts the recorded message. Why did it frighten you?'

But the fembly had run off across the fields, wobbling from side to side, her skirt pulled over her eyes, her spiky heels almost tripping her. Alice sighed pityingly and continued on her journey.

About an hour later (as measured by Harmony time, which was the only time she knew) Alice arrived at a clearing. Gathered in a circle was a large group of memblies dressed in splendid robes of purple and gold and wearing exotic headdresses shaped like pyramids, embroidered with gold and silver thread with insets of rubies and emeralds. Other memblies wore black jerkins over black tights which showed off their knees and calves to great effect. There was much hammering and sawing and Alice saw that a platform was being erected. Two femblies sat with the memblies. They were clad in grey from head to toe in a sort of wraparound garment and only their eyes were visible.

Alice sat where she could not be seen and reflected on her adventures to date. She closed her eyes and dozed for a while.

She was awakened by the sounding of a brass gong. 'Bedoyng, bedoyng,' it went booming through the clearing and echoing off the nearby woodland. One of the memblies climbed on to the platform, which was now ringed by ropes, and called in an important voice: 'Round one, fembly Hussy and membly Fuzzy. Partners in crime. Destroyers of the constitutional right of the majority. Annihilators of the sacredness of the membly, without which no life is possible. Begin.'

Into the ring stepped two little people wearing striped bodystockings, each carrying a long pole with tinkling brass bells. The two femblies in the gathering let out long sighs and all the memblies turned and stared at them with such mournful expressions that the femblies covered their eyes and were totally silent.

The membly who had made the announcement and who was known, Alice later discovered, as the deaferee, called out again, 'Begin.'

One of the creatures backed into a corner and began to sob bitterly. 'I don't want to begin,' it said. 'I want to go home.'

'There, there,' the other said. 'You can go home if you want to. Let's make up again.'

'Bedoyng,' went the brass gong. 'Round one to membly Fuzzy. Two tickets to the football final on Saturday.' The membly looked distinctly pleased. With that the fembly rushed out with her stick and bells and hit him on the top of the head, making an entrancingly musical sound as she did so.

'Oooooh.' The membly gathering groaned and the pyramid hats wobbled precariously. 'Foul,' shouted the deaferee. 'Round two to membly Fuzzy. Two pints of pinnis per day per month.' A glazed look came on the membly's face. The fembly tore out from her corner and hit him again with the brass bells, which this time sounded like a chorus of singing birds. The sound filled the clearing and the two femblies in the gathering covered their ears with their hands and began to rock. One of the pyramid-hatted heads leaned over and tapped them reprovingly on their shoulders. The tap seemed to shrivel them up because, to Alice's amazement, their grey garments folded in on them as if there were no bodies there at all. But she thought she could see the bright beaming eyes somewhere in the folds of the material. The membly in the ring began to grow bigger. He stuck his chest out and said, 'You're getting uppity.' The gathering roared with approval and the creatures beat the ground with their sticks and feet and bashed the heads and hats off each other. They looked so ridiculous that Alice longed to laugh out loud, but she stifled her mirth for fear of being discovered. The fembly in the ring looked amazed at the membly's remark.

'Uppity?' she squeaked. 'Uppity? I never heard of such a thing.'

'Bedoyng,' went the deaferee's gong. 'Round three to membly Fuzzy. Two questions in a row, one denial.'

There were strange rules to this boxing match, Alice thought. It looked as if the odds were in favour of the membly. If that were the case what was the point in the exercise? And where were the matches? And who was to be matched? It occurred to her that perhaps it was a mismatch. It was some kind of contest for a mismatch. But who would win? And what would the prize be?

At this point the fembly seemed to become calmer. She appeared to be thinking. Then she dropped on to her little round belly and crawled into the centre of the ring.

'I pray justice,' she said. 'In the name of the great and good I pray justice.'

There was a deadly silence then and the deaferee looked to the gathering for guidance. A few of the pyramid hats shuffled some papers and began to leaf through pages with intense concentration. One of them signalled to the deaferee, who descended to consult with him. There was much nodding and shaking of heads and finally the deaferee came back to the ring and called out, 'Round four to membly Fuzzy. Inappropriate appeal.'

Membly Fuzzy looked worried, but in spite of his worried look he was beginning to swell. By contrast, the fembly was shrinking much in the same way that the two femblies in the gathering had shrunk, but her shrinkage was totally visible because of her striped body stocking which now hung loosely around her, the feet trailing like a tail as she crawled back to her corner.

Alice could not contain herself any longer. She leaped to her feet and cried out, 'Where is your justice, you stupid people? Why are you shrinking the femblies? If they shrink any more there will be nothing left.'

She expected an angry response but all she got were some strange stares and more shuffling of paper and a few sniggers from the back rows. The most senior-looking membly stood up, took off his pyramid hat and intoned in a deep voice, 'That is the general id-ee-aa. The shrinkage of the femblies in the boxing ring is the ultimate and only good. It is therefore not moral to decide the fate of either being. All has been preordained. It is in the nature of things that femblies shrink and memblies swell. So it has always been and so it shall always be.'

A great peal of thunder followed his words, the sky darkened and huge drops of rain began to spill on top of everyone.

'Rounds five and six to membly Fuzzy,' shouted the deaferee above the thunder peals. 'Rain stopped play. Drag away the body.'

There was not much left to drag away. The poor little fembly bodystocking seemed completely empty and the poor membly was so swollen and stuffed-up he could scarcely walk. He rolled over on his side and began to groan. The deaferee leaned over and took his stick with the bells on it and laid it beside the fembly's stick, which had suddenly sprouted little flower-heads. Out of one of the flower-heads poked a tiny nose and a bright pair of eyes.

'Mamba, famba,' called a plaintive voice. The membly rolled off the ring and down the hill and the deaferee followed him, collecting raindrops as he went.

'Mamba, famba,' called the creature. But no one was listening. Alice climbed into the ring and picked it up.

'Mamba, famba, famba, mamba,' cried the creature again and again.

'That's all I need,' said Alice disapprovingly. 'I

suppose you'll have to come along with me.' She slipped the creature into her pocket and followed everyone else out of the clearing.

Chapter Four

It seemed that all were making for a giant building. Alice had never seen a building which reached so high that she had to crane her neck to look at the top of it, or indeed to look at the azure about it. She missed her friend, the fembly, because she might have told her the purpose of this building and the reason for its size. In Harmony Isle, Alice's native country, no building was allowed to predominate over the contours of the land or the height of the inhabitants. In Harmony Isle, and Alice sighed to remember it, everything worked in relation to everything else. Actions have consequences. Words have echoes. Thoughts penetrate mountains. Ripples in the pond make storms in the ocean. These were part of the credo of Harmonisers. Yet here in Thunderland, each set of actions seemed to have its own value and its own set of rules without their being in any way interlinked. Except, thought Alice, for one interconnection. The femblies always came out the losers although they themselves did not seem to believe so. And after Alice had witnessed the mismatch and seen the bloated condition of the membly she began to wonder if some memblies were not also losers, in fact if not in theory.

The road to the building had been long and rocky. On the way there were many potholes and even chasms. To Alice's horror several of the fembly creatures, especially those who travelled in groups, fell into these chasms and were lost forever. Some howled loudly as they fell down and threw up to their comrades fragments of their clothes or pieces of paper with strange words scrawled on them.

The braver among the femblies reached for these remnants and passed them secretly on to each other. Once or twice a membly caught hold of one and he either read it and tore it up in contempt or burst out laughing and passed it around to his group. Sometimes he passed a fragment to femblies with much shaking of his head and waving of his stick and the femblies then laughed dutifully. Some of the memblies went so far as to try to push a few femblies into the potholes, and as far as Alice could see they might have succeeded in pushing one or two into the chasms.

By this time Alice noticed a change in herself which worried her but about which she could do little. She was beginning to shrink. Either that or she was being pressed deeper into the ground beneath her. It was an unfamiliar experience and she had to find a coping mechanism for it. She murmured the ritual prayer she had learned as a child from her grandmother, who had learned it from her grandmother, and so on back through the generations. It was the emergency prayer: 'I am who I am. I am the imperishable. I am the impregnable I. I am the creator and giver of life. I am the one.' To her relief, as she chanted it she stopped shrinking. But she had already lost a few inches and she determined that as soon as she escaped from this crowd, which had by this time grown hugely, she would concentrate on regaining height. The strange thing was that, as Alice had shrunk, the little wembly creature had grown, and at one stage, as Alice stumbled over a pothole, it actually fell out of her pocket with a screech of annoyance.

'Mamba,' the creature said, 'you are leading me the wrong way.'

'I'm not leading you at all,' said Alice. 'I'm just giving you a ride so that you can get safely to wherever you want to go.'

'You're my mamba,' said this creature, who only a short while before had been a bright little pair of eyes and a plaintive voice. 'If things go wrong for me, it's your fault.'

'My fault!' Alice exclaimed. 'I do my best for you. I carry you in my pocket for this long journey. What is my fault?'

'I didn't ask to be born,' said the creature importantly. Alice burst out laughing at the impudence of it and everyone around looked at her in annoyance.

By this time the crowd had reached the front door of the building. This was an ugly, iron-framed affair with memblies' heads carved on it. In the forecourt were sculpted statues of memblies on horses or standing on plinths with their arms raised, or holding writing tablets. There were hundreds of them. As Alice was pushed through she felt a hand reach for hers and turning around saw to her great relief that it was her fembly friend.

'Isn't it exciting?' the fembly said. 'At long last. To think I have lived to see this day!'

It was an odd thing to say, Alice thought, because the fembly had quite obviously not lived very long. However, Alice's need for information was great.

'Why are there no fembly statues?' she asked.

'Oh, but there are,' said the fembly proudly. 'Look!' and she pointed to a corner where a sad-looking statue holding a membly baby stood in an archway covered with plants. 'There is the She who represents us all.'

'Yes,' said Alice. 'But she doesn't look like you. Is she like you? Was she one of you? Will your statue be in the forecourt some day?'

'I don't do important things,' said the fembly. 'Femblies never do important things. Only people who do important things have their statues in the forecourt.'

'What are important things?' Alice asked.

'You are very stupid,' the fembly said angrily. 'And I warned you about asking too many questions. Lucky for you, everyone is so busy today that they are not being picked up. Otherwise you'd be for it, let me tell you.'

At that precise moment a gong sounded. Over the front door a brightly-coloured platform unfolded and on to it stepped a membly wearing a shiny coat with lots of brass objects on it and lots of coloured ribbons.

'Who is he?' Alice asked.

A membly beside her gave her a very dirty look and hissed, 'Keep quiet. He is the Hero Boss. He will guide us into the right path and bless our righteousness. For we are the chosen ones. We who follow our hero have moved on to the right path and travel to our destiny.'

'It was a very pot-holey path,' said Alice, 'and full of chasms. There were many accidents on the way.'

'There are always a few mishaps, said the membly. 'You have to accept those. Look at all the buttons on our Hero Boss. He has had to push many into chasms, though his heart broke to do it, so that he could head us to our destiny.'

'He had better not try to push me into a chasm,' said Alice, 'or he'll get what for.'

The membly's attention was distracted by the appearance of another creature, a fembly who was ushered out by various attendants and who stood beside the Hero Boss looking a little bewildered but smiling. At the sight of her, all the femblies started cheering and the memblies scratched their little polls in confusion and then the Hero Boss cheered, so they all cheered too. Everyone cheered like mad. Alice thought this was great fun and she joined in the cheering.

This is a great day,' the fembly said. 'This is the greatest day in my life.' Alice could not but be glad for her, but she thought she could not have had many great days if journeying on such a terrible road and losing so many of her friends in order to stand cheering in front of a big building with a coloured platform was a great day.

'She has made it to the platform,' the fembly said. 'She will have a say.'

'I should hope so,' thought Alice, although she did not say it aloud because she had already had a few dirty looks and was afraid of shrinking any more. Added to that the wembly creature was by now up to her waist and was actually trying to climb up on to her back for a better view.

'Please get off my back,' Alice said politely.

'I will not,' said the wembly. 'Your back is my ladder and up it I will climb.'

'You'd better let it climb,' said the fembly, 'or you'll get an attack of the guilts. Terrible cramps. You can be in bed for weeks with them.'

To Alice's horror, the little wembly had already succeeded in climbing half-way up her back and was clinging on to her for dear life. Alice wriggled and squirmed and tried to shake her off, for she found her weight oppressive and painful. She hadn't minded carrying the creature in her pocket. In fact for a while it had been quite pleasant and in an odd way comforting. There were moments on the journey to this place when

Alice had experienced what she realised was the Thunderland sensation of loneliness. The wembly creature for a while alleviated this loneliness. But half-way up her back, and heading fast for her shoulders — that was going too far. She reached one arm behind her back to grasp the creature's legs. Imagine her outrage when her so-called friend gave her a whack on the arm and said, 'None of that. You've got to do your duty. We all had to do it.'

'What has that to do with anything?' asked Alice. 'What you do is your business. What I do is mine.'

'You've got a thing or two to learn,' said the fembly. 'and the sooner you learn it the better. You have to learn to shape up or formcon. We started very young. It will be much harder for you but I'll help you.'

'No,' said Alice. 'Please do not. It sounds extremely painful and I do not wish to formcon.'

'Like it or not,' said the fembly, 'you'll learn.'

Alice noticed with some bewilderment that the closer they were to the building, the more arrogant the fembly became. Where was the clingy pathetic creature who had wept such tears at their first meeting? Where was that little spark of something, something, something? Alice could not quite think what, but it was something. And then Alice realised that for the first time since she came to Thunderland she had forgotten what she was going to think.

The wembly was climbing on to her neck and had stretched her little paw up to Alice's head. Alice put her own hand up to push it back and she felt, just above her ears, a few feathers. She pulled one out and she remembered the story about the femblies growing feathers instead of brains. She looked around to see if anyone was staring at her, but no one noticed. Instead everyone was staring intently at the fembly on the platform. What would she do or say, Alice wondered.

What could she do or say with the Boss Hero standing so close to her with all his brass buttons! Perhaps she will sing a song, Alice thought hopefully, or do a somersault or show them all how to fly. It will be really good, Alice thought. And if she does something really good I am quite sure my feathers will stop growing and my memory will come back. What was the word I wanted? What was the word? What was the word?

And then she remembered. Spirit. The fembly, even in her tears, had spirit. But before she had time to consider the change in her friend, the fembly on the platform began to speak. As she opened her mouth all the memblies clustered around, looking terribly solemn.

'We will begin again,' said the fembly. 'Let us begin again.'

It did not seem to Alice to be a particularly significant remark and yet it was greeted with something amounting to awe. Beside Alice, her fembly friend said with satisfaction, 'You see. It was worth coming this far.'

The Boss Hero then opened his mouth. 'This is a great day,' he said. 'The fembly has had a new hair-do. She has a new skirt. The fembly looks good. I salute the fembly.' And everyone started cheering again. At this point the wembly managed to reach Alice's head; she pulled herself up by the feathers which were growing rampantly on poor Alice's head and joined in the cheering. Alice could feel herself sinking, sinking into the ground, being pressed down deeper and deeper. As she was going down the wembly leaped off her head, shouting, 'Thanks for the ride, sucker,' and vanished into the crowd.

Alice felt another sensation now. Not loneliness. She had identified that one. It was like loneliness. It was loss. A loss sensation. What was this loss sensation? It was the grief most feared in Harmony Isle and Alice groaned as she realised that she had come to face it. She was suffering the terrible disease of alienation. And as she lay, trampled into the mud, while all around her everyone cheered and jumped for joy, she noticed that the feathers were beginning to fall out of her head. Well, she thought, out of every evil may come good. My attack of alienation is rotting my feathers. Good, thought Alice. Very good. I'll get out of this mess yet.

Chapter Five

Alice lay for a long time as the feathers withered and fell around her. They were soft downy things and she thought sadly as they left her head that they might have given her comfort if she had learned to grow and harvest them properly. They could have been used to stuff a mattress and she might have lain on it all summer, eating ice-cream and drinking beer and smoking grass. And this weird thunderland world could rocket around her as it pleased and she would not even notice it.

Strange thoughts, strange thoughts. Idly she picked a feather and began to suck it. A drowsy numbness enveloped her. The noisy crowd faded away into the distance. Grey clouds drifted over her head. She seemed to be absorbed into them, floating with them over the babble of confusion below. So far away…so wonderfully far away. She was suspended above herself and could just faintly see her own shadow lying on the mud as snowflakes fell and fell and covered her.

It was winter in Thunderland. First the rain came and everyone complained of being wet. Then it grew cooler and everyone complained of being frozen. Then it grew dark and everyone complained of being depressed. For a month or so no one noticed Alice lying asleep in the corner of a field covered with a white substance. Then one evening a child returning from school poked at her with a stick. Instantly a flame of light leaped upwards towards the dull sky and a low humming sound could be heard all over the field. Naturally the child screamed as children will do when they are afraid. People came running from houses nearby. They gasped when they saw the mound. An ancient fembly fell on her knees before it, crying, 'At last, at last! It has come at last!' But before anyone could discover what had come, she keeled over and died.

Then two young femblies approached the mound cautiously. They knelt in front of it, turning their heads towards the flame. Their faces shone, reflecting brightness, and their lips moved, although no words came. Around them, their families and friends shivered in awe. Some fell on their knees as well. Others began to chant aloud:

> *Oh mighty one.*
> *Oh brightness of brightness.*
> *Oh bridge over the river of sorrow.*
> *Oh path through the forests of despair,*
> *Oh singer of songs still to be sung,*
> *Oh gatherer of tears.*
> *Oh comforter of the abandoned.*
> *Oh saviour of the femblies.*
> *Oh...Oh...Oh...*

Their voices hushed as if they heard something. They fell, femblies and a few memblies, on to their knees and covered their faces with their hands.

Alice stirred sleepily in her strange cocoon. The voices around her lulled her back to sleep. Heavy as her eyelids were the sighs from the crowd. Heavy and numbing and sleep-inducing. She slept and dreamed of Harmony Isle. She dreamed of the great sister and the little brother and the quiet corridors and the green plains and the wheat waving silkily and the trees blossoming and the rivers with their leaping fish and the skies with their plumed birds and the golden roads winding through the ruby towns and the cities of amethyst and pearl. She dreamed of the outstretched hands and the smiling faces and the music in the tongues of her friends. As she dreamed these dreams the flame of light leaped higher. It illuminated the field and the houses and the muddy lanes around.

Pilgrims came from miles around to marvel. Some said they were cured of their fears and pains. Some came to scoff but went away quietly. Then one morning a great machine arrived with a horde of memblies aboard. They put up a sign forbidding unauthorised persons to enter the field. Everyone had to leave. They made a gate and put a membly in a box beside it. He took pictures of the mound and the flame and began to sell them. One or two femblies protested and said they had discovered this place and what about the two visionaries who prayed there every day.

'We will explain it all,' the membly said. 'We have written it down and we will pass it on to you. Then you will understand it too. We will call this mound a clarification centre. It is better for you if we tell you the right way of things so that you do not fall into error. This is the word of the boss. This is the rule of the law. Be patient and all will be revealed to you in time.'

The membly charged a fee to look over the fence. Reluctantly some femblies and memblies paid. As the first coin changed hands a strange thing happened. The flame of light flickered. Over the next few days it flickered frequently. 'It's going out,' the people cried. 'It is dying. Your charge is destroying our flame.'

'Nonsense,' the membly said sternly. 'You don't know what you are saying. Idle chatter. Get back to your places.

Buy the book. Buy the book. All will be explained.'

But no one wanted the book until an edict was issued commanding everyone to buy it and to learn it by heart. A day was fixed by which time every household had to have a copy of this book and produce it as evidence of their good intent.

However, before that day came, something else happened which the femblies would talk about for many years to come and on which they based much of their new thinking. The flame of light went out. The snow-flakes melted and Alice, stirring sleepily, woke at last.

It was early morning. She shook herself free of the mound and sat up to look around and to get her bearings. A pair of round black eyes stared into hers and a familiar voice said, 'I thought it might be you.' It was her friend the fembly.

The fembly looked pleased with herself. 'I guessed it was you all the time,' she said. 'All this fuss and I knew. I knew all the time.'

She began to chortle in a funny chokey way, rocking herself to and fro in glee.

'What fuss?' Alice asked. 'There is always a fuss about something in this Thunderland. A great to-do and a much ado about nothing. It would make you grow hairs in your ears if you thought about it too much.'

'I *have* hairs in my ears,' the fembly said crossly. 'And I certainly don't think too much. It's not allowed. Well, *my* kind of thinking isn't allowed.'

'What kind of thinking is that?' Alice asked.

'Sideways,' the fembly said with a curious touch of pride.

'It seems to me,' Alice said, 'that everyone and everything is sideways in Thunderland.'

'You haven't learned anything since you slept,' the fembly cried, clapping her hands to her hairy ears. 'There you go again, being critical. Why are you so critical?'

'What a funny thing you are,' Alice said with amusement. 'One must have a criterion by which to judge. By my criterion, Thunderland is sideways.'

'Critical, critical, critical,' the fembly cried woefully. 'There is too much criticism.'

Alice consoled her. 'You mustn't take it personally. I don't wish to offend you. Please calm yourself. Rest for a moment in my cocoon. There is not much of it left but it may refresh you.'

The fembly's pinched yellow face brightened and her hairy ears perked up as she looked at the welcoming shape of the cocoon.

'I will lie down for a few moments,' she whispered. She had scarcely uttered the words when alarm bells rang so loudly that Alice thought her eardrums would burst. The fembly leaped in fright and clapped her wizened little hands to her own ears. A voice rumbled menacingly, 'It is forbidden to rest out of sleep time. Penalty for breaking this rule may be severe. You will be given three warnings. If the third warning is not heeded proceedings will follow. I will repeat this message.'

'There is no need to repeat it,' Alice called impatiently. 'We hear and understand. The fembly will not break the rule.' Indeed the poor fembly had leaped back from Alice's cocoon, which was now rapidly shrinking. She stood as if to attention, all her sharp features tense and alert.

'There is such a performance about everything,' Alice grumbled. 'I cannot think why those bells have to go off. And why is it so wrong to lie down when you are tired?'

'I don't know why I have anything to do with you,' the fembly said with a sigh. 'Don't ask any more questions or you will set the bells ringing again. I am mortified enough as it is. It will take a long time to live this down. I shouldn't have listened to you. You are bad company. You are leading me astray.'

'If that is the case,' Alice said agreeably, 'there is not much point in our being together. Shall I leave first or will you?'

'Don't be so disagreeable,' the fembly said. 'I didn't say anything about leaving. I will simply have to be more careful when you are around. I...' She paused for such a long time that Alice thought she had finished and she opened her mouth to say that she would be careful also. But the fembly continued, 'I like to be in your company. It is more dangerous but not boring'

'What is "boring"?' Alice asked.

'Do stop,' the fembly said. 'Do not ask another question.'

'That will be difficult,' Alice said. 'If I need to ask directions...'

The Voice rumbled again. 'You will not need to ask any questions in Thunderland. Everything is explained.'

Alice looked around in amazement. The fembly was covered in confusion.

'I am terribly embarrassed,' she said. 'You have drawn the Voice on us. He will go everywhere we go now. We will never get rid of him. It happened me once years ago.'

'Ten years and three months and twelve days ago,' the Voice reminded her solemnly.

'Yes, yes,' the fembly muttered. 'I know.'

'And six hours,' the Voice droned huskily.

'Yes,' the fembly said. 'Yes.'

'And twenty-seven point two three seconds as of *now!'* Do nothing,' the Voice continued amicably. 'Think nothing. Say nothing. I will do all for you. I will be your guide and mentor.'

'What will she have to give you in return?' Alice asked suspiciously.

'Never you mind, missyknowallsmartypantsfromforeignland. Keep your nose out of our affairs or you'll find yourself without an olfactory organ. Hee hee hee.' The Voice seemed highly amused and pleased with itself.

Alice tried to get a fix on it so that she could direct her gaze towards it but it appeared to hop all over the place, at one moment seeming to emerge from the fembly's ears, at another floating above her head, sometimes coming between them and sometimes chortling away in the distance over the hills.

'Oh dear, oh dear!' The fembly wrung her hands. 'I'm stuck with it.' Alice looked sympathetically at her and was about to offer a suggestion as to how they might get rid of this unwelcome companion when she caught the fembly giving a sort of coy look around. She had an odd little smirk on her face, one that denoted pleasure, or so Alice had observed in her short acquaintance with her.

'I believe you like the Voice,' Alice said.

'I do not,' the fembly cried indignantly. 'I hate it, hate it, hate it.' She stamped her pointy toes in fury.

'You called, Madam,' the Voice called merrily. 'Call me and I am yours.'

'Go away and lie down somewhere. Cool off,' the fembly said.

'I thought you were afraid of the Voice,' Alice said. 'You seem to like it.'

'Beggars can't be choosers,' the fembly said. 'It's all

right for you. You've got everything. What have I got? I'm a sort of norfan. A person without a person. The Voice is better than nothing.'

'Isn't it a kind of spy?' Alice asked.

'Yes and no, yes and no. It can be controlled.'

'Oh control me,' the Voice cried. 'I long to be controlled.'

To Alice's astonishment the fembly began to chuckle. 'I'll try,' she cried. 'Let me see you first.'

'Coax me,' the voice murmured, right beside Alice's ear.

'Please please please,' the fembly whispered.

'Just for a minute then. Watch.'

As Alice and the fembly stared, a white tooth appeared, floating in the air above them. Then a red lip with above it the faintest trace of a moustache. Then another tooth and a lower lip.

'Do put in all your teeth,' the fembly cried. 'I don't like the gaps.'

'OK,' the voice said. 'Here I am in all my glory.' And a fine set of strong white teeth flashed between the two red lips under the smidgen of a moustache suspended half-way between Alice and the fembly.

'Thank you,' the fembly said politely. 'I have seen enough. You may go now.'

The upper lip curled. 'Don't push your luck, femmy,' it said, a shade too familiarly, Alice thought. The fembly stayed silent, her eyes now hooded so that her expression could not be seen.

The lips closed over the teeth in a sort of pout. Alice was fascinated. She had never seen a floating mouth before. She was not sure that she liked it. She stared intently at it and it suddenly sucked on something and vanished, muttering something about a right little gobshite, which Alice was pretty sure was something rude. But she was beginning to get used to the rudeness mixed with the strange defensiveness which was the most notable attribute of the people of Thunderland.

'Is it gone?' the fembly whispered.

'I think so,' Alice said.

They looked around cautiously. There was no sign of the mouth. 'A nasty experience,' Alice said.

'Mmmm,' the fembly replied in a non-committal sort of tone. 'If you say so.'

'I did say so,' Alice reminded her politely.

'Oh, of course, of course. Don't make a song and dance about it.'

'That sounds fun,' Alice said. 'I think it would make a great song and dance.'

'You think too much,' the fembly said, as if she were repeating a lesson.

'It is not possible to think too much,' Alice contradicted her. 'Thinking is an absolute in itself. It cannot have limits or boundaries. One either thinks or one does not. It is neither good nor bad, merely a function of the cerebral cortex.'

'I know plenty of stupid people,' the fembly cried indignantly. 'They certainly don't think.'

'You are confusing thinking with judgement,' Alice explained patiently. 'The two are not incompatible but may be mutually exclusive in given circumstances. Judgement, logic, the ability to reason and to come to rational conclusions, are functions of thinking but are by no means the only functions. One may think without judgement although one cannot make judgement without thinking.'

'Isn't that just what I said?' the fembly asked crossly.

'In a way, yes,' Alice said, 'and in a way, no.'

'There are times,' the fembly said, 'when I can get too much of you.'

'One cannot have too much of a good thing,' Alice said.

'Yes, you can,' the fembly cried. 'If you eat too much strawberries and cream on your birthday, as I did, you can get sick.'

'Then either it was not a good thing in the first place, because its potential was not essentially good, or it was a good thing to be sick and it was intrinsically a good thing in the first place. In the latter case you did not have too much of a good thing and in the former you had too much of a potentially bad thing.'

The fembly stepped back a few steps and looked at Alice, who had a faintly glazed look on her face. The fembly put her hand to her mouth and began to weep.

'Oh dear, oh dear, oh dear,' she cried. 'Oh dearie, dearie, wearie me.'

'What are your complaints, my little treasure?' came the booming Voice, softened as if speaking from a great distance.

'My friend has changed.'

'Your friend has got a minor attack of memblitis,' the Voice explained. 'She might, if she studied hard, get a degree in bullosoffy.'

'How did she pick it up?'

'Who can tell? She is a stranger in these here parts. She may not be immunised. There are occasional plagues of bullosoffy, minor outbreaks, or major epidemics, depending on the weather. Have you noticed a lot of heavy cloud lately?'

'Now that you mention it, yes,' the fembly said thoughtfully.

'Give her time and it will pass. Pose no more questions. Make no more contributions. Eliminate literary allusions from your conversation. Concentrate on your toenails or those delectable hairs in your ears and a cure will shortly be effected.'

The fembly sat down obediently and crossed her bony knees, staring intently at Alice all the time. Alice looked benignly back.

'I wonder if I could catch it,' the fembly murmured.

'Hoo hoo. Whoooo,' the Voice bellowed. 'I hardly think so, my little pea-brain. You still have too many feathers.'

'I have no feathers,' the fembly said indignantly.

'Explain your hairy ears then,' the Voice shouted triumphantly.

'Why should I explain them?' the fembly said. 'There is nothing to explain.'

'You asked a question and you gave an answer. Both to yourself at the same time. That could be an offence.' The Voice had become deeper and more solemn. The fembly began to look scared again.

'Alice. Alice,' she cried feebly. 'Alice. Alice.'

But Alice did not answer

'Ahh,' the Voice said. 'She has gone. She has gone with the wind to make her name.'

'I want her back. I want her back,' the fembly cried passionately. 'Please send her back. You like me, don't you. Please send her back.'

Oh what a thunderous Voice there was then. Rumbling and rocking and shaking the moon and the trees and the clock towers, whipping off the tails of cats and the ears of dogs and owls' beaks and the long noses of the vegetable Aspedillas. So loud was the Voice, so far echoing and deep-sea-reaching that storms shook the lobsters from their shells and the crabs from their seaweedy caverns. Alice was blown upside down and lay like a hewn tree, legs stiff, hair spread out around her head. The poor fembly was whipped up into the air and blown off course to anywhere. Alice, through her daze, heard her faint despairing cry above the shouting, denying, angry Voice. 'Alice. Alice. Alice.' But she could not answer.

Chapter Six

For the third time since her arrival in Thunderland Alice lay oblivious to membly affairs and Thunderland opinions. All her energies were focused on stabilising her harmony and recovering and adjusting to her inner essence. The assaults on her person were beginning to affect her. Withdrawals were bound to be more frequent. As she came back to her senses she was very aware of the danger she was in. Too many of these oblivions might lead her to total withdrawal and final alienation. She knew that she must fight hard if she was to survive her sojourn in Thunderland and make her way back to Harmony Isle.

By the time she had staggered to her feet, the fembly was out of sight but not out of mind. In her head Alice could hear her cry, like a miniature bell sounding its message over and over. 'Alice, follow me, follow me. Find me, find me. Search the highways and the byways, the low ways and the slow ways, the upwinds and downwinds. Seek for me in underground caves and in the hollows of trees. Look for me wherever there are sighs and sounds, where music is hidden, where lost treasures wait to be discovered. I am where birds nest. I am where dogs dig. I am where the Karkadile makes her lair, in muddy banks and wildflower meadows. I am where lemon balm and thyme scent the air. I am where roots grow deepest and shadows are thickest. Look for me in starshine. Look for me in moonbeams. Look for me in sunlight. Find me where the bridge of rainbows joins the worlds of air and earth. Alice. Alice. Alice.'

I must go, Alice decided. This bell will never stop ringing in my head until I have found the fembly. And then she heard a sigh of relief, very loud and appealing. 'You may leave my head now,' she cried. 'I hear your message. If you do not leave my head I will not be able to think and I will not be able to find you.'

She waited for an answering tinkle. Perhaps there was the merest sound. Then there was nothing but the sound of her own heartbeat.

'Thank heavens for that,' she said. 'Bells in my head I can do without. Where to start. That is the problem. Which way does the wind blow?'

She wet her finger and held it up. It chilled in the south-west direction. She pointed her nose SSW and sniffed. The Karkadile might not be the easiest to find in its muddy lair. She would have to ask for directions.

Alice trudged through the field, in which the spring daffodils were now blooming. At the other side of the fence some femblies clustered, looking suspiciously at her. One of these, unusually fierce in appearance, had multicoloured feathers sprouting from her head, decorated with caterpillars and birds' eggs. She walked towards Alice, scowling.

'I have heard about you,' she said menacingly. 'You are a disrupter of the fembly lifestyle. You ask questions.'

'Yes,' Alice agreed, smiling cheerfully. 'I do.'

'We do not like questioners in our place,' the fembly said. 'We have had plenty of questioners here in the past. We know how to deal with them. Some of them we tied to the apple cart because they upset it and spilled all our apples.'

'Did you pick them up?' asked Alice.

'We did not pick them up,' the fembly said fiercely.

'They turned into cider and the vegetable Aspedillas drank them through their long noses and they sang all winter and none of us got any sleep.'

'I am sorry about that,' Alice said. She thought carefully about how she might continue this conversation without asking a question. A suggestion which would enable the femblies to avoid a similar disturbance might be useful.

'Perhaps next time if you picked the apples up when the apple cart was upset you could store them and make use of them.'

The fembly drew herself up to her full two feet.

'We do not need you to tell us what to do. We were doing very nicely until you came along. And if our apple cart is upset it is up to us to decide how to downset it.'

'Sometimes,' Alice said carefully 'Apple carts get too heavy and they upset themselves.'

'Our apple carts never get too heavy,' the fembly said proudly. 'Our system does not allow it.'

'What is a system?' Alice asked, forgetting herself for a moment.

Another fembly came pushing forward, half-hiding behind the first fembly, but looking twice as fierce. She wagged a finger at Alice and said, 'You have taken my cousin away from us. We saw her going with the wind. Who knows what will happen her now? No one has ever come back from the windy quarter of our land. It is all your fault. You should be locked up. You should keep your mouth shut.'

'I certainly will not,' Alice said. 'And I don't think you could make me. I did not take your cousin away. The Voice had something to do with that.'

The femblies looked apprehensively around and then

gathered together in a small circle, their heads touching one another. Alice noticed that many had feathers sprouting from their ears and over their eyebrows. Some were painted bright colours. They looked very attractive. Others had objects tied to them. At the back of the group a very small round fembly had not joined in this circle. She sat examining Alice intently. Alice was pleased to be looked at with such interest. This fembly seemed to be older than the others, although with femblies it was hard to tell what age they were.

She carried a small oval dish with a lip at one end. She held it carefully. It was an ornate dish, in fact one of the most elaborate and well designed objects Alice had seen so far in Thunderland.

'You like my dish.' The fembly nodded to Alice.

'I do,' Alice said.

'It is a tear holder. I am the tear gatherer,' the fembly said. 'I was appointed last moontime. Tears have become scarce in recent times and the Boss has decided to save them in case we have an emergency. Do not ask,' she wagged a finger warningly, 'what emergency. Any emergency may arise at any time.'

That was very obvious to Alice. She thought they lived in a state of constant emergency but she did not think it was an appropriate time to say so.

'I am now the chief tear gatherer. I have many helpers all over Thunderland searching out tears. Fembly tears are precious but membly tears are even more valuable because they are almost extinct. They are a protected species. Anyone wasting or throwing away tears can now be punished. The Boss has written an important document on the new value of tears.'

'I saw a pool of tears somewhere,' Alice said helpfully.

'Where?' the fembly asked excitedly.

'You have asked a question,' Alice pointed out.

'A one-word query does not count,' the fembly said. 'Especially when it relates to location. I repeat. Where?'

'Far away,' Alice said vaguely. 'I think it belonged to my fembly friend. We swam in it with the funns in the funnery.'

The femblies whinnied. Alice did not think she had said anything funny. To make certain, she repeated what she had said. They whinnied even louder. The older fembly said knowingly, 'All funneries were banned many years ago. Funns have been extinct for centuries.'

'The funns I saw were not extinct. But they were underground somewhere.'

At this piece of information the older fembly gravely shook her head at Alice and put a finger to her lips. She waved her dish commandingly at the group and told them to go back to their houses or they would be accused of gathering together without a licence. One said haughtily that she had a licence to gather and she would produce it if necessary. But the others obviously did not, because one by one they left the group and returned to their homes. The haughty one looked around for a while as if testing something. The older fembly muttered something to her about her leggings being too tight for her or her being too big for her leggings and the fembly replied that she had friends in high places and was allowed to get too big for her britches. The older fembly lifted up her tear dish, high above her head and cried out, 'I am the tear gatherer. Who will defy the tear gatherer?'

In the distance came a rumble of thunder and Alice thought, here we go again, here comes big bully boy, the Voice in person. The great controller.

The warning was enough for the fembly. She wiggled her tight leggings and ran. The older fembly said smugly, 'I knew that would fix her. She'll have to go back into her box now and she'll have to stay very quiet for about a week or the Voice may track her down.'

'Will the Voice track you down?' Alice asked.

'Not when I have the office of tear gatherer. This is a civil appointment. Pensionable. I'm allowed free travel to the Karkadile and I have immunity to harassment by the Voice.'

Again there was a faint rumble and the older fembly seemed disconcerted. 'What did I say just then?' she asked rather timidly. 'I am becoming forgetful.'

'Harassment,' Alice said. 'You mentioned harassment.'

The rumble was louder this time.

'Oh stop,' the older fembly cried. 'Don't mention it again. Stay very quiet for a while.'

She carefully put the dish on the ground and lay down beside it, pulling her brown skirt up over her face so that it was covered. She beckoned to Alice to do likewise. Alice obeyed. They lay still as the rumbles continued faintly over the horizon, moving here and there as if searching for a quarry. Finally they faded and there was complete silence. Alice waited until the older fembly gave her the signal to move. They sat up together. The older fembly polished the tear dish with a silken cloth she had tied to her waist. As she polished, one of her own tears fell into the dish with a great plop. She heaved a sigh and said softly, 'Out of evil may come good.' Then she stood up. 'Let us go,' she said. 'You can be assistant tear gatherer. You will not get a pension but you may get a training for something.'

They walked along the hard black road with its many

holes half-full of water. Alice had become adept at keeping out of these holes after several minor accidents in which she had twisted an ankle or fallen on her wrist. The holes were being filled in as they passed but Alice knew from experience that they were getting only temporary cover. Great black machines making an enormous racket were busy going to and fro. As they worked Alice noticed the machines themselves were making new holes which one membly had the task of filling. He used an implement with a large flat head. Alice thought it was a kind of support because every so often he leaned heavily on it and mopped his forehead. He was breathing in dreadful smelly fumes from the machine and his face was beginning to turn an oily green colour.

'That poor membly has a hard time going behind the machine,' Alice remarked.

But the fembly seemed quite indifferent.

'I am sure that if you approached him he might have a tear or two,' Alice continued.

'Those kinds of memblies don't have tears,' the fembly said. 'And even if they did,' she wrinkled up her nose, 'they would be of a low quality.'

'Why?' Alice asked boldly, aware of the one-word query rule and knowing she was following it.

'I find you increasingly difficult,' the fembly said crossly. 'In our new dictionary, which is just now being compiled, there is a list of three-letter words which may be used only on special days. Why is one of them. In fact,' she added proudly, 'under a new directive, one into which my organisation has had an input, the list will limit the use of words offensive to the general good, by which all of us, memblies and femblies, will benefit, and will add words of scientific worth and sociological and logical value.'

'I would like to hear some examples,' Alice said politely.

'I can't give them to you just now, just like that, without any preparation. These are important, important.' She flapped a hand vaguely. 'You know, important...' she paused for a long while and said triumphantly, 'things.'

'Important things,' Alice repeated, more puzzled than ever. Uneasily she felt again a reeling of her sense, a dizziness, a rapidly rising enervation. She clutched her head and sang as loudly as she could the nursery rhyme taught to her by her foremothers:

> In the land of the Karkadile.
> Live the lords of the leery smile,
> Tarry awhile, tarry awhile
> Then leave them to wallow in guile.
> In the land of the great pretender
> Forget not to remember
> Keep your thoughts alert as defender
> And leave by the end of December.

Her song rolled over the hills, echoing almost as far as the thunderous tones of the Voice. Alice and the older fembly stood listening to the echoes and to other sounds that accompanied them, the sounds of bluebells, of grass-blades sharpening, of leaves falling, of secret laughter. Alice felt better.

'Let us move on,' she said briskly. 'You are not making much progress with your tear collection. You need to ask someone.'

'I cannot ask too many,' the older fembly said. 'If I use

up my quota of questions I will be completely land-lubbered. And then there will be grigs on the screen. The observers will find me on their channels and I will be notified of aerial disturbance. That in itself is a minor dismeanour. Upsetting the telltale-all-vision, from which information is dispersed. I am taking the trouble to explain this to you so that you will not make the mistake of asking. I hope you appreciate my kindness.'

'I am grateful beyond words,' Alice said. 'But I would like to help you find some precious tears. As I recall, if we turn to the left just ahead of us we might be near the place where I fell into the funnery. Those rocks look familiar. It was here I had my first sighting of a herd of memblies.' She was about to say that around the corner was her boat and that she might if she had enough provisions set sail for Harmony Isle. Native caution prevented her from revealing this information. It was a struggle to keep it in her head. The older fembly seemed a sensible creature but, Alice reflected, femblies as much as memblies were affected by the extreme conditions of Thunderland. She could not entirely trust even the little fembly whom she had learned to love. She would keep her counsel and make her move off the island when all the signs were in her favour. Wind, weather, ways and wishes.

'My fembly friend wept tears,' Alice remembered. 'And no one collected them.'

'They were probably tears of self-pity,' the older fembly said. 'Not what I would call high quality.'

'All tears are to some extent tears of self-pity. We weep for our own sorrow at the sorrow of others.'

'I am seeking tears with passion. Tears for loss, tears for love, tears for joy, tears for relief, tears for another's anguish without self-regard. These are the purest tears.'

'We have plenty of those in Harmony Isle,' Alice said. 'They are so common no one bothers to collect them.'

'Of course,' said the older fembly. 'What's rare is wonderful. I understand that.' She turned and for the second time looked intently at Alice. This time there was a touch of speculation in her gaze which made Alice uncomfortable.

'I could trade your tears for copies of the book of our system.'

'I did not know femblies could trade.'

'There are a lot of things femblies do, sub judice and sometimes with surreption. Femblies operate an economic system which benefits all without the trauma of having to face acknowledgement or reward. Memblies are better equipped for these things. It has always been so from the beginning. And it always will be so to the end.'

A determined creature, this older fembly, Alice thought, beginning to be bored and wishing she had not made the decision to accompany her on her search for tears.

As they travelled on, the road became narrower. Ahead of them was a fork with a signpost pointing to the right saying, 'Karkadile Lair may or may not be here.'

'That is a peculiar sign,' Alice remarked.

'Not a bit,' the older fembly said. 'That leads to the initiate training centre for people who are on the live register.'

'I suppose everyone who is alive is on the live register,' Alice said, thinking to herself that she was sure to be right about this deduction.

The older fembly whinnied and Alice felt her heart sink. She was wrong again.

'Only those who are registered alive are on the live register,' the older fembly explained, as if talking to a person of low intelligence. 'You have much to learn. I hope you do not intend leaving us for a while. It would not be in your best interests or, for that matter, in ours.'

Alarm bells went off in Alice's head. This older fembly, she realised, was a spy. She was not interested only in collecting tears. Her job was to keep an eye on Alice and perhaps even to prevent her return to Harmony Isle. I must play along with her, Alice thought. I must pretend to follow the rules. But I must continue to keep my own counsel. I wonder if she can read my thoughts. She practised a little telepathy, transferring an innocuous thought about the grass growing ahead of them in the centre of the road with the sign. But the older fembly made no comment and Alice realised with relief that femblies had not yet developed this very useful, though potentially dangerous form of communication. Alice herself was only a novice because she had not completed the ten years of study required to mistress and control the gift.

The older fembly stopped at the fork in the road.

Underneath the sign two juniors were playing with stones, piling them up on top of one another and then knocking them down. One child cried out that the other was cheating and hit her with a stone. The child put her hands to her head and began to rock to and fro.

'You should get some tears here,' Alice advised. 'Tears of rage.'

The older fembly held her dish under the child's eyes, telling her what she was about.

'What are tears?' the little creature asked plaintively. 'Do you have to be on the live register to have tears?'

The older fembly seemed both embarrassed and angry at the questions.

'These creatures,' she explained to Alice, 'are not normal juniors. They are the wanderlusts. They make their own rules and do not follow the question rule. We ignore them as much as we can but they are becoming a nuisance. I expect we will have to take action of some sort. However, that is not my department. Someone else can sort that one out.'

The other child stood up and called out defiantly, 'I know where there are plenty of tears. I saw them myself. How much will you give me if I show you?'

'I'll tell you what I'll give you if you don't show me,' the older fembly said. 'A clip on the ear.'

'I have a clip on my ear already,' the junior boasted, pointing to a metal object hanging off his right ear.

'That is nothing to the one you'll get from me,' the fembly said. 'It will pull the ear off your head.'

'You and who else?' the little junior membly cried, dancing mockingly up and down. 'You are only a fembly. I don't have to listen to you.'

At that the older fembly knelt on the road and lifted up her hands calling out, 'Great Voice, I need you. Come to my assistance.'

Thunder rolled and a commanding Voice roared out, 'What do you want, oh gatherer of tears?'

'A clip on the ear to keep this creature in his place.'

To Alice's horror an enormous metal clip suddenly appeared and in spite of the screams of the junior membly attached itself to his ear. He threw himself on the ground, kicking and yelling. Alice went over to comfort him but he kicked out at her and she drew back only just in time. As soon as she could, she decided, she would leave this tear gatherer who could mete out such terrible punishment to a junior rebel and she would make her way to her boat. She longed for peace and tranquillity. She wished for order and harmony. When would she ever find it again?

Chapter Seven

After the incident with the junior wanderlust Alice and the fembly travelled in silence. The road ahead of them narrowed and led into a thicket where there was a sign, 'Double walkways'. Alice had seen several of these notices before but having no occasion to follow them, she thought little more of them.

As they entered the thicket she realised that she was caught up in a frenzy of activity, with creatures rushing to and fro through the bushes, knocking each other down and blowing whistles. The older fembly was instantly infected by the same panic and, roughly pushing Alice in front of her, shouted, 'Get in line.' She was just in time, for Alice was almost knocked over by a large membly sitting on the back of a wheeled object, waving a printed notice with one hand and blowing his whistle with the other. As he passed her, Alice was almost asphyxiated by the fumes coming from his wheely and she had to stop to recover. The older fembly poked an impatient finger in her back to urge her forward.

'You cannot stop here,' she called above the noise and the smells. Alice had no wish to stop. All she wanted to do was to get out of this walkway, but once on it there seemed to be no turning off. The thicket grew darker as bushes with thorny spikes reached out to prick her. Ahead of her many weary travellers jogged as if on a treadmill from which they had no escape. They were burdened with immense back-packs containing all sorts of goods and materials. Some had packets of food; others had the flat toolheads like those used to fill in the road holes; others again carried nozzles with mouthpieces. Alice determined that come what may she would ask a question of somebody about the purpose of these.

They seemed to travel for hours through the foggy darkness of the thicket. At times they went around in circles, an even more dangerous procedure because of the large numbers of creatures going round these circles but coming from different directions. Occasionally Alice thought they could branch off into a quieter place but always the older fembly behind her poked and prodded her along.

At last they came to another fork in the road. Some of the travellers ahead turned off to the left, others to the right. Slightly to the right of the right turn was a narrow unsignposted track. Alice managed to glimpse a tattered cloth hanging on a bush and bearing the letters Ka before she turned swiftly and ran on to the track, missing by inches a team of memblies who were running from the opposite direction. She heard the older fembly cry out as she turned through the main left-hand route. Alice was relieved to be rid of her and glad that she had taken the decision so quickly to turn into this unfamiliar, uncharted territory. Uncharted, that is, apart from the signpost Ka which might or might not point the way to the fabled Karkadile's lair.

She found herself in a grassy dell. Gnarled and knotted trees grew beside a pond on which water lilies floated, their faces turned towards the sun which shone through the branches of the trees. Gone were the fumes, the fog and the noise of the walkway. A rubbery creature, half-plant, half-animal with a long, nozzle-like nose siphoned water from the pond.

'Good day,' Alice said politely.

The creature turned mournful eyes towards her.

'Good day to you too, my dear,' it said in a husky croak.

'You must be Alice. I, my dear, am the Aspedilla. I left the sign for you. The older fembly is too slow on the uptake. She is a poor navigator. I knew you would make the instant decision necessary to find me.'

'I am glad I did,' Alice said. 'I have heard the femblies talk of you.'

The Aspedilla shook his head impatiently. 'They will never forget the cider incident. I enjoy cider. It stays in my nozzle for a long time and never goes to my head. I make music with it all night long. Like this. Listen.'

He lay down on the ground and blew bubbles through his long nose. Then he began to burble, playing tunes as if on a flute with a pleasant, watery, bubbly sound.

Burble, burble, gurgle, gurgle, gurgle went the Aspedilla.

Alice applauded and the Aspedilla bowed his thanks.

'You see,' he sighed. 'No one appreciates my music. I make much better music with cider but it is so hard to find upset apple carts these days that I am quite deprived. Long ago femblies upset the apple carts regularly. But, oh dear me, those days are gone, alas. And now I have very little cider for music making. You see,' he explained, 'it gives a tartness to the tone and allows for greater flexibility of range. I often take a tonic solfa to help clarify the tunes. But nothing, nothing compares with the fermented juice of the apple newly upset from an ancient apple cart.'

'I am sorry for your trouble,' Alice said. 'In Harmony Isle we make music from everything. We make it from the reeds that grow by the rivers, from the willow and hazel branches, from anything through which the wind may blow and from everything on which we can beat a rhythm.'

'For myself I do not care to beat a rhythm, the Aspedilla said. 'I once saw a rhythm beaten to death and I have never recovered from the shock. I am quite sure it has shortened my life.'

'I am sorry to hear that,' said Alice. 'It is better to put these sad experiences behind you.'

'I have been to counselling,' the Aspedilla said proudly. 'And I managed to make several tears which I have saved for the tear gatherer. They are safe here in a box. These are genuine tears. None of your self-pity things. And not overly emotional either. I would save only the best.'

'What did you do in counselling?' Alice asked.

'Why, nothing. That is why one goes to counselling. One goes to do nothing. Then one cries. Then one comes away.'

'Did it make you feel better?'

'Better or worse. Who knows which way the wind blows when the Aspedilla blows its nose,' the creature said wisely.

Alice couldn't help laughing and after an initial look of surprise the Aspedilla began to laugh too. He burbled and wheezed beside the pond and took out a large flowered handkerchief to wipe his streaming eyes. He shook the handkerchief with an elegant paw, then began to wave it in a circular motion over his head. As he waved, the flower patterns produced leaves and stems and roots and when he dropped it on to the ground the handkerchief formed a canopy under which the newly sprouted flowers rooted and grew.

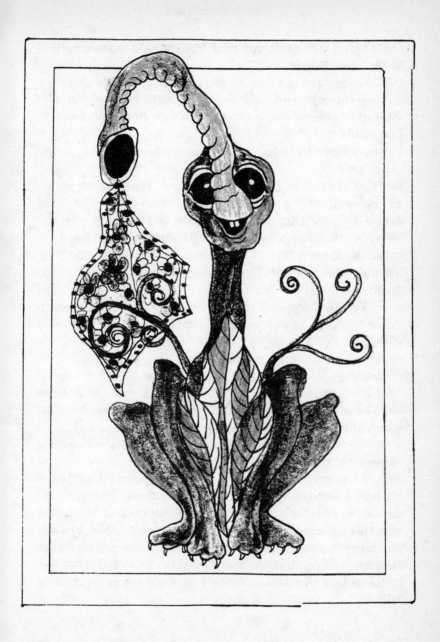

'That is a wonderful trick,' Alice said admiringly. 'I wish I could do it.'

'You are not an Aspedilla, my dear. Which of us by taking thought can add to our stature by one cubit? I cannot become an Alice. You cannot become an Aspedilla.'

'In Harmony Isle we do many things by thought,' Alice said.

'You are not in Harmony Isle now. There is not much to be gained by idle boasting,' the Aspedilla said languidly, stretching himself on the grass and beginning to nibble the flower heads. 'Would you like some lunch?'

Alice did not like to refuse but neither could she bear to pull the beautifully coloured flower heads which seemed to shrink back as the Aspedilla pulled them towards his long red throat. One of them appeared to Alice to look appealingly at her for help. Boldly, she decided to act.

'I see something in the pond,' she said, hoping to distract the Aspedilla. She succeeded over and above all her expectations. The creature leaped up in a fury, immense thorny bristles rising on his neck and legs. In place of his mournful expression there was now a glare of sheer hatred. He stared anxiously at the water for several minutes, during which time Alice managed to pull up the flowers gently by their roots and replant them in a sheltered spot behind a large leafy plant. The flowers curled up like kittens with their mother and snuggled into this new parent, who covered them protectively with her hairy leaves. The handkerchief, now deprived of its flowery decoration, withered and shrivelled like an autumn leaf and was absorbed into the ground where it lay.

'You scared me,' the Aspedilla said reproachfully lying back again and producing another handkerchief, this time with birds and bees painted on its surface. Alice thought that she could not bear to see these lovely creatures materialise only to be devoured by his insatiable appetite.

'I must go,' she said, standing up and shaking her skirt down.

'Must you indeed? he remarked, leaving his handkerchief down for a moment and eyeing her.

'Yes, I must.'

'Must thou art and must thou bee. As honey sucks me I suck thee,' the creature murmured.

'I don't understand,' Alice said feeling a little apprehensive at the change in his tone of voice. She took a step forward only to find her leg clasped in the thorny grasp of his left foot. She shook herself fiercely but could not escape. As she watched in horror, the formerly gentle creature removed his long nose and replaced it with a nozzle and mouthpiece rather similar to those she had seen being transported on the walkway.

'You rescued my lunch,' he said. 'But you will make a good substitute. I have never had an Alice before. You look pretty delectable to me. A cute little piece, I think. I can have a pleasant evening's entertainment with you.'

'I am quite tough,' Alice said, fighting for time. 'And I am not as delectable as I look.'

'Do not underestimate yourself,' the Aspedilla said. 'You followed my sign. You made yourself available. Do not tease me only please me and all will be well.'

By this time his foot had dug deeper into the flesh of her leg and the blood was oozing through her skin.

'I thought you were a nice creature,' she said,

beginning to feel dizzy and weak.

'What is thought? I ask rhetorically,' he said. 'You did not think. You assumed. Never assume. Never presume. Or you may be consumed by the Aspedilla.'

'Before I am consumed,' Alice said, sitting down again and placing a hand on top of his thorny paw. 'I would like to know something more about you. How, for instance, did you get your name?'

'What a bore,' the Aspedilla sighed, mopping his brow with the handkerchief. 'You are only going to delay matters. However, the laws of hospitality forbid me to ignore your question and oblige me to answer it as best I may. I am the only, the true, the original Aspedilla. There are some poor imitations with shorter nozzles and fewer functions. But none, I may say, without boasting, are as perfect in form and substance as I. I am distantly related to the turrited turrilites who are themselves related to the ammonites. In former times I believe we lived wholly in the warm seas of our ancestral estates. My relations have become fossilised, alas, and many are now collectors' items.' At this melancholy thought, he wept copiously into his handkerchief, which he then squeezed into the pond, not for a moment relaxing his grip on Alice's leg.

'You may have come across some of my relatives in your travels. They regularly feature on the airwaves. They are now airers of things. Views, opinions, notions of all sorts. Not my style of thing—I am too artistic. I sit by my pond and meditate on life. But enough of this idle gossip. Come here, my little chickadee.'

There was only one thing she could do, much as she hated to do it. Alice screamed as loudly as she could and then bit deeply into the imprisoning paw. As it happened, the scream would have been enough, for the Aspedilla leaped backwards and fell head over heels into his briny, tear-filled pond. He dropped his handkerchief as he rolled in. Alice did not wait to see if he could swim. She picked up the handkerchief, intending to use it to bandage her leg, and ran as fast as the painful limb would allow, out of the grassy dell and on to a forest path. Behind her rose the sobbing, burbling sound of the Aspedilla singing or crying—she could not be sure which and she did not care. This was as narrow an escape as she had had so far in Thunderland.

The forest path continued for a few miles. It eventually opened out into a pleasant meadow. At the far side she saw a bank and guessed that it might hide a stream. Sure enough, when she had hobbled over to it there was a clean flow of water. She sat down and dipped the handkerchief into it and then wrapped it over the painful leg. She lay down beside the reeds at the edge of the stream and gathered her thoughts.

Life in Thunderland was becoming more and more dangerous. The further into it she travelled, the less resilient she became. All these dangers and unpleasant creatures were beginning to sap her natural energies. If this continued she might lose all her resources, her innocence, her optimism, all the gifts that were the birthright of every one born on Harmony Isle. If she lost these, she might never find her way back. Why, she wondered, had she allowed herself to be lured on to the walkway? Why had she taken that turning to the Aspedilla who had almost destroyed her? She had been totally deceived by him, by his languid air, his music and his pleasant talk, his tricks with flowers and birds. He had only wished to subsume her into himself, to make her one with him as he had made the poor flowers he had managed to eat before she rescued them. Are there no pleasant creatures at all in Thunderland, she asked herself, apart from her friend the fembly? And here, in spite of herself, poor Alice began to cry by the side of the stream. As her tears flowed, she undid the handkerchief from her leg and mopped her eyes. When the handkerchief was drenched, she shook it, as the Aspedilla had done, and instantly all the birds and bees that had been mere painted creatures burst into life and into flight.

Except for one bird. It was a feathered but flightless bird, with bright black eyes and golden plumage. It perched on Alice's hand and sharpened its blue beak on her nails.

'Excuse me,' Alice said. 'I am not here to act as your beak sharpener.'

'You will do. You are not perfect but you are all I have at the moment.'

These words were uttered in a piping tone but there was something about them that reminded her of the Aspedilla.

'I am the Aspedilla's springer off,' the golden bird said. 'I am mind-reader and also doer of good. You rescued me from my voracious past but what do you need me for? I did not expect to find you lying asleep by the bank of the famous river Limnach down which the invaders of our land came astral years ago.'

'I want to find my way home,' Alice said.

'And the sooner the better by the looks of you. First you must know my name. I am Bird.' He perked himself up and ruffled his feathers proudly.

'I can see that,' Alice said.

'What do you mean?' Bird piped. 'You would never have known had I not decided to inform you. This was secret information, known only to me.'

Well, thought Alice, I am not going to argue with this bird. If it can get me out of this mess I'll agree to anything it says.

'A wise decision,' Bird said.

'Can I not think anything without you reading my thoughts,' Alice asked.

'But of course not,' he replied. 'Unless you have a Thunderland thought-switcher which is available only at the Karkadile's lair. And yes, I am going to bring you there. Hop on my back.'

This golden creature, feathered and beady-eyed, sat on her hand, sharpening its beak on her finger-nails, suggesting she would be able to sit on its back and that it would be able to bear her weight!

'Just do it, please, and let's not waste any more time,' Bird piped.

'How will I get on your back?' Alice asked.

'The usual way. And if I were you I would not ask any more questions. Questions, questions, questions. The most boring things in the world are questions. Especially when one doesn't know the answer and most especially when one does because, because, one then has to *give* the answer.'

Oh, Alice thought impatiently. This bird is just like the Aspedilla.

'I *am* the Aspedilla.' The thing laughed hilariously 'But I would rather be back in my own place instead of having to do this for you. Hurry up, you lazy thing, or you will lose the chance and I won't ask you again.'

Alice, feeling foolish, put one leg on each side of the golden-plumed Bird. In an instant she was airborne. Up and away towards the blue sky, her legs encased in downy cushions, her arms wrapped around the silky neck of her sky flyer. It was a long time since she had felt so exhilarated. Up, up they soared. Faster and faster they flew. Far below Alice saw the dark, gloomy tracks of the walkways almost covered by the smoky fumes of the wheelies. Hundreds of figures ran hither and thither, dodging each other. She almost thought she could hear their whistles. Then below her, the shining river Limnach curved around settlements and meadows and coursed through shadowed valleys. As they flew over one of these valleys she heard a loud bang. Her carrier shuddered suddenly and cried out, 'I've been shot, I've been shot.' Suddenly it lost height and began to plunge towards earth. All around her were mountains and from these mountains came spurts of fire and loud explosions. She clung on to Bird, whose voice was faint as he said fearfully, 'We have entered the war zone. I did not know the war zone was here. Sorry, sorry, sorry.'

It was too late for apology. How they dodged the whizzing flames of fire coming at them from all directions Alice could not tell. She buried herself in Bird's feathers as they landed heavily beside a ruined house. Alice shook herself off Bird's back. He lay, badly wounded, but beginning to shrink back to his normal size. It would be easier to help him if she could carry him to a safe place. Soon he was the small, blue-beaked bird she had first seen. She picked him up and put him in her pocket. All around her were the charred roofs and burned-out remains of a settlement. There was no sign of life, only bundles of clothes which looked as if they might have belonged to memblies and femblies. From every hill around her came noise, much greater than that in the walkways. Noise, smoke, fumes and fire were everywhere. As she stood an explosion louder than any so far brought a huge lump of metal past her ear and into the shell of the house beside her. It burst into flames and burned to the ground in an instant. Alice ran towards the shelter of the lower part of the hill.

Chapter Eight

Alice hid under an overhanging bush while around her and below her the noise of warfare continued. In her pocket Bird trembled.

'Be comforted,' Alice spoke silently to him. 'We are not finished yet. We will wait until this blows over.'

'We might die,' Bird wept. 'I am not ready to die.'

'Neither was I,' Alice reminded him. 'But that did not seem to worry you.'

'You are alien,' Bird said. 'And I am an alien here. It changes the rules of the game.'

'I don't think much of these rules,' Alice said, not for the first time. 'The rules will have to be changed.'

Bird said, 'Rules are never changed. Rules are rules. Unchangeable. *De facto*. Infallible truths.'

'Now you sound like a membly.'

'I am confused,' Bird sighed. 'I preferred it when I was a genuine Aspedilla. It's all your fault. I'm sorry I did not subsume you when I had the chance.'

'You would be wise to keep your complaints until you are better. Your life depends very much on me, since you are now in my pocket,' Alice said, squeezing him to make clear his dependence.

'My day will come,' he piped. 'Even a Bird has its day.'

Their conversation was stopped by the approach of heavy, tramping boots and strange voices. Alice pressed herself against the side of the hill, making herself as nearly invisible as she could, concentrating hard on becoming one with the shrub behind her.

Two outsize memblies wearing saucepan lids on their heads stopped in front of her. They carried the nozzle-like implements she had seen being transported in great numbers. One put his down and began to clean it as he spoke.

'This is a lovely weapon,' he said in a tone of affection. 'It was drunk with blood. I was able to dispose of forty-six little cruts to-day. I got a fembly crut right in the middle. You should have seen her go. Woooo!'

'That is more than I got,' the other said jealously. 'Which do you prefer getting, the fembly or the membly cruts?'

'I like to get them in different ways,' the first membly said. 'I have a few tied up for us tonight. That will give the lads some fun.'

The other suddenly began to sniff. Sniff, sniff, sniff went his bulbous nose. 'I smell something!'

'Do you smell a crut?'

'I can't be sure. There is something funny around here.'

Alice closed her eyes and put her hand tightly over the shaking body of Bird. 'My sisters,' she prayed silently. 'My sisters in Harmony Isle. My dear little brothers. Succour me in my hour of need. This is my first prayer. I want to go home. Let me find my way home.'

It was not to be. The first and larger of the two memblies turned around and pulled the bushes to one side, exposing her to their view.

'Look what I have here,' he shouted triumphantly. 'It looks like one of them.'

The other peered. Both had red eyes painted in the middle of their foreheads.

'Good day, Red Eyes,' Alice said, hoping she was

using the correct address.

'By Bozo, she's big,' the second membly said. 'I've never seen one as big. Is it a crut? Is it a proper fembly? What is it?'

'Who cares,' his companion said. 'Let's blast her anyway.'

With that Bird hopped out of Alice's pocket, chirping sweetly. 'I am neither a fembly nor a membly. I am a Bird. Be good to me and I'll be good to you.'

Alice thought this was a feeble plea to make to two obvious monsters. She was not surprised when they began to cackle in a loud and raucous parody of laughter. It would have been wiser of Bird to stay mute.

'So she has you in her pocket, has she?' laughed saucepan lid head number one. 'We'll soon change that. Hop in here, my lad,' he said, taking off his saucepan lid and holding it out for Bird. Obediently, Bird jumped in.

'Out of the pocket and into the saucepan lid,' saucepan lid head number two chanted. 'We'll have his liver and guts for breakfast and we can casserole the rest for dinner.'

Squawk. Whether indignation or terror lent him wings Alice could not tell. All she saw was Bird exercising his one good wing and one bloody one, flapping upwards toward the eye of saucepan lid head number one. Straight into its red centre went his sharp beak. Then there was a yell of rage and pain as the monster staggered backwards and fell off the edge of the hill and into the pit of violence below. He vanished into a mêlée of explosions and flashes of light. Bird half-flew, half-scrambled up the hill away from his tormentors.

Alice saw saucepan lid head number two take aim with his nozzle. Chip chop cherry, she sang, as she kicked out with all her might. The nozzle went flying into the air. The monster gaped in amazement at her as she knocked him off his heels, over the ledge, in the wake of his former companion.

'Sorry about that,' Alice called after him. 'But you asked for it.' And she began to climb up the hill in the track of the terrified Bird.

She caught up with him after twenty minutes or so. He was still half-flying, half-climbing, all the time snuffling and grumbling under his breath. 'Why did I bother talking to that creature? Why did I not stay where I was, in my own place, where I was safe, where I could eat the tormibilas to my heart's content, where I could change my shape and size to suit my mood or the weather? Why did I fall for that creature?'

'You did not fall for me,' Alice reminded him. 'I shook you out of the Aspedilla's handkerchief. Only for me look where you would have been.'

'I would have been safe and sound with my friend the Aspedilla who was always a kind master and a faithful ally and who taught me all I know about the winds and ways of the Great Lake.' Bird began to sob bitterly. 'He warned me against tangling with strange femblies who would lead me into temptation and danger.'

'If it weren't for me,' Alice said, 'you'd have been swallowed whole by the Aspedilla. I rescued you.'

'I didn't ask to be rescued,' Bird said. 'That was your idea. And look where it got me. I just this minute escaped with my life. I was almost, almost, almost…' He began to choke and sob even harder so that he could not utter the words.

'A casserole?' Alice suggested helpfully.

'You fiend!' Bird shouted. 'You fiend from the regions

of nether. Never come near me again. I will warn everyone against you. I will tell the world how you nearly destroyed me. I feel inspiration already.'

Although Alice was used to being surprised by the creatures she met in Thunderland, she found Bird's next action beyond all imaginings. From his wounded feather he pulled out a quill which he sharpened with his beak, dipped in the blood still oozing from the injury inflicted in the war zone and began to write on a nearby stone.

This is the tale of Bird, he wrote.
I am a bird who must fly on one wing.
I have a tragic song to sing.
I have dipped my beak in the well of despair.
I have tasted the tears of the one with long hair.
I have supped with the greatest in the land.
I have casseroled monsters with a single hand.

'Are you not making a mistake here?' Alice said, leaning over his shoulder and pointing to the last sentence. 'Should that not be the other way around?'

'Do I look as if I was casseroled?' he challenged her, puffing his feathers out and stretching his good wing.

'It did not happen,' Alice said. 'But it was more nearly happening you than the monsters.'

'See this,' Bird said, tapping his pretty beak. 'Did you or did you not see me gouge out the red eye of saucepan lid head?'

'You pecked it and knocked him off balance.'

'I'll knock *you* off balance if you keep giving me lip,' Bird said fiercely. 'You're getting too big for your boots. There are ways to deal with you.'

From far below them in the pit of the valley came

horrible screams and yells as the monsters with their saucepan lids waged war on one another and on everyone and everything that happened to be in the way. And here was Bird, full of feathers and fury, writing an epic to celebrate his temporary release from danger.

'Would your time not be better spent,' Alice suggested 'trying to rescue some of the wounded down there? Perhaps you could call the Aspedilla to give you a hand. Or arrange a truce and a new set of rules so that wars become outlawed and anyone who breaks the rules is banished.'

Bird put down his quill and looked thoughtfully at her. 'Yes,' he agreed, to her surprise. 'We could banish all undesirables to Harmony Isle.'

I walk in a land of treachery, Alice thought sadly. She turned away from him saying, 'Write your epic if you must,' and continued her climb up out of the horrors she had witnessed. As she went she heard him mumbling her last words 'Write an epic if you must,' and adding:

> *Though words and wonders turn to dust,*
> *I am Bird, the poet's king.*
> *Beware the thrust of my rhyming sting.*
> *The words of doom lurk in my breast.*
> *Who treats with me should take good rest.*
> *Effort and toil and the pangs of fame.*
> *Are the fate of those who play my game.*

'Well,' thought Alice. 'A rhymster is a strange class of a Bird. He can make his ditties while the world burns.' A horrible thought struck her. She had picked up some of his rhythm. There was a danger she might catch the terrible plague of poesy herself. A nursery rhyme or two was all right in its place and in Harmony Isle there were certainly many scribes who interpreted wisdom for the workers and who even, on rare occasions, read their epics in the public place. But to produce them at the drop of a hat, in the midst of grief and anguish, was new to her.

But then, grief and anguish were also new to her. She had been protected in Harmony Isle from the stress and angst of Thunderland. For a moment or two she wondered if this was a bad thing or a good thing. It was a different kind of a life here but it was in its own way an interesting one. She had had experiences unknown to her sisters and little brothers in Harmony Isle. Surely, surely, these would be of some benefit to her. Here she was struck again with the thought that Thunderland philosophy was entering her psyche. One of its favourite maxims was that no experience, however bad, should be wasted. Was that why Bird felt obliged to write his epic?

Puzzling over this new idea, Alice continued on her journey upward out of the valley of war. As she climbed, the air became clearer and the heather more brilliant with bells of rich purple and pure white blooming in abundance. Along the ditches she crossed in her journey were star-shaped plants of brilliant blue that seemed to reflect the sky, which was now dazzling and sunny.

The steep slope levelled out and she was able to run lightly on its springy surface. Wonderful scents filled the air, reminding her of her homeland. Perhaps this place had once been like her own place. Perhaps, oh terrible thought, her own land might one day become like this one, with its rules and taboos and its strange inconsistencies, its saucepan lid men, its noisy walkways, its overpowering Voice, its femblies with feathers sprouting from their heads.

Up here on the top of the hill she seemed miles away from any Voice. Up here there was complete silence. It was the first real silence she had known since she came to Thunderland. No birds sang, no Voice thundered. There was only the faint whisper of the wind ruffling her hair.

Thunderland had some good places in it. It was only a question of finding them, Alice thought.

Feeling relaxed and happy she scrambled over a rocky mound and realised she had reached the summit.

Below her on the other side of the hill a track led to a round, stone building with smaller stone buildings, shaped like beehives, clustering in groups of four and five. As she approached, she heard music and the sound of children laughing. At last she had found the happy side of Thunderland. She was so relieved she ran quickly down the hill and climbed over the first stone wall on the perimeter of the enclosure. Inside it was another stone wall and she easily scaled that one. But as her foot touched the ground a bell pealed loudly, the children's laughter was snuffed out like the flame of a candle, a net dropped over her and she was dragged, kicking and struggling, to the nearest of the small stone buildings.

As she lay, furious at being caught yet again, she noticed a door opening from the building. Marching towards her were two femblies, dressed in short tunics and carrying buckets of water. They stood over her, examining her silently, then walked around her, prodding her as was the custom of so many in Thunderland but this time with a little more kindness.

'I think it's a species of fembly,' the second said. 'Very large and plump and with much hair, but definitely a species. We'll bring it inside. But first, do you speak?' she said, addressing Alice with polite determination.

'Of course I speak,' Alice said. 'I didn't get here without being able to speak.'

'That presents us with a problem,' the first fembly said. 'How did you get here? This place is unknown to all but the secret few.'

'I came via the war zone,' Alice explained.

'Then you must have suffered,' the femblies said gravely, looking at one another.

'I saw suffering,' Alice said. 'But I did not experience it.'

'We cannot keep you here if you have not suffered,' they said. 'We need all our places for those who have suffered. You will have to go away. But now that you have seen our place we must be sure that you will not reveal it to anyone. This is a a place of safety and it must remain so.'

'I won't tell anyone,' Alice promised, wishing they would undo the net. 'I feel uncomfortable tied up like this.'

'Can you give us evidence of your good faith?' one asked. 'What are you called?'

'I am called Alice and I come from Harmony Isle.'

'We know nothing of any Harmony Isle. Only the harmony we try to create in this chaos,' the other said and they both laughed as if it was a joke.

'I would appreciate a place to rest for a while,' Alice said, 'on my journey back to my own place.'

'We are on the same journey. But we look for our own place here. Now we must wash you of your memory of this place,' they said. 'We apologise,' and they threw their buckets of water over her, chanting, 'Water of life cleanse her of all impurities. Wash her clean of memories of us. Send her on her way in good heart.'

Alice closed her eyes as the liquid gushed over her. She licked her lips as it ran down her face and over her mouth and chin. It had a sparkly fizzy taste and made her feel happy. She sat up, realising as she did so that the net was gone. She looked around. She was in a bare field with no sign of stone buildings or enclosure or any femblies. But straight in front of her was a large painted sign with the message 'Turn left for the Karkadile. Visitors Welcome.'

Obediently and full of curiosity, Alice turned left.

Chapter Nine

She walked along a grassed-over track bounded by hedges and banks full of many kinds of flowers. Wonderfully coloured butterflies fluttered over the blossoms. A sign at the side of the track read 'Green Road.' As she looked around her, Alice realised that she was climbing on a cliff above the sea. Below her were puffins and sea birds that circled and flew continually in and out of their nests on the cliff face. Far below she could just make out the curve of the bay into which she had sailed on the eventful day of her arrival in Harmony Isle.

Where was her boat? If she could find it she would set sail immediately. She was long enough in Thunderland. It was time to leave. She had learned as much as she needed to know and more that she did not wish to know. The sounds of the war zone left unhappy echoes in her ears.

Already her head, once so erect and challenging, had begun to settle into her shoulders. And as if from the weight of this heavy head, her shoulders were beginning to droop. What was the cause, she asked herself. It was the fashion of Thunderland people. But what was the cause?

A scarlet butterfly which had been resting on a white blossom flew in front of her. Alice followed as it fluttered into the ruin of an ancient building and paused at the arched doorway. A plaque declared it the meeting place of an extinct race of religious femblies. The butterfly settled on a pivoting stone near the doorway. It swung open to reveal a passageway leading underground. Alice entered and immediately the stone closed behind her.

All around her were jewel-like colours so bright they gave light to the passageway. Down, down went Alice, far down under the cliff. She could hear the booming of the sea getting louder and louder and then fainter and fainter. Eventually she reached a courtyard which led into another passageway on which was a sign, 'Straight on to the Karkadile.'

And there in front of her was a domed building shaped like an enormous seashell. At its entrance sat an ancient fembly examining her fingers. As Alice approached, she called out, 'Welcome, Harmony person. The Karkadile is waiting.'

Alice entered the building hesitantly. Water lapped outside the windows and multi-coloured sea creatures floated by. The light was an incandescent green. Alice seemed to bathe in it. Her head began to lift and her shoulders to straighten. She stretched her arms out and felt herself upheld by the buoyancy of the atmosphere. And then in the corner she noticed a pair of sleepy eyes contemplating her. They were embedded in a creamy flesh which rested on a great pearl shell. Below the eyes was an orifice from which came a flute-like sound which at first seemed to make no sense.

Alice sat down and listened politely. The sound was music and yet not music. It sang and did not sing. It spoke and did not speak. It was the sound of silence. It entered her heart and told her that she was welcome.

'Thank you,' said Alice.

At this the creature stirred and floated towards her, blinking its eyes as it moved. It began to talk in its flutey voice.

'You have seen our sadness,' it said. 'You have heard the Voice. But you have experienced little.'

'I am only a visitor,' Alice said. 'I am here only for a short while.'

'A short while to some is a long while to many,' the creature said.

'May I ask if you are the Karkadile?' Alice said.

'You may,' the creature nodded. 'But I may not answer. It is true that I am called the Karkadile. But it is also true that I am not called the Karkadile. Some say the Karkadile lives below the sea. Others say she is old as the oceans and older than the firmament. I say the stars were born before the Karkadile came.'

It closed its eyes and slept.

After waiting a while Alice stood up and looked through the sea windows with interest. A scaly-winged fish winked an eye at her as it passed. Another opened its large mouth in a grin full of sharp teeth. Hundreds of minute fish darted swiftly through the water, moving in shoals of rainbow colours. Looking through the windows was like looking into a shifting kaleidoscope where colours interchanged and re-formed in myriads different patterns. The effect was slightly hypnotic and Alice felt herself nodding and about to join the Karkadile in its sleep when she heard its flutey voice coming from just behind her.

'You have questions to ask,' said the Karkadile.

'I do not know where to begin,' Alice said. 'When I first came here I had many questions but because I was not allowed to ask them my curiosity has become blunted and I now do not know which questions to ask.'

'You may wish to reach the state of wisdom in which an unquestioning mind may rest.'

'I would be afraid to rest my mind,' said Alice. 'How would I use it if it was always resting?'

'The mind is receptor. It cannot receive if it does not rest. How can the great Creative Being initiate the flow of stars if it does not rest?'

And here the Karkadile closed its eyes and fell asleep. Alice turned again to look through the window at the sea creatures. She gazed and gazed. After a while she noticed the same sea creature passing by and looking steadily at her. She began to look out for this creature, counting the numbers of fish who swam between its appearance. After each one hundred and twenty-five fish the same creature appeared. Are they swimming in circles? Alice wondered. Is this not the mighty ocean, but an enormous fish bowl?

'You are getting warmer and warmer,' the Karkadile said behind her. 'In fact you are getting so warm I am beginning to feel quite breathless. Please clap your hands and call for a glass of air.'

Alice clapped. Two femblies, tunic-clad, the very same femblies who had trapped her in the net when she had discovered the safe house, now appeared with a large flagon. They attached it by a spout to the Karkadile, who inhaled thankfully.

'A wonderful draught of elixir,' it said. 'So soothing. I am refreshed. I will show you what you need to be shown.'

'Please show me the safe house and tell me why it is there.' And they were there. Back in the clearing with the stone beehive huts and the children laughing, but this time there was no net. There was no sign of the Karkadile but its flutelike voice spoke to her as she walked into the building.

'This is a place of learning. Here we learn about

danger zones.'

'I have seen the war zone,' Alice said.

'Watch,' said the Karkadile's voice.

Alice was in a circular room where femblies and their children sat and watched a scene being enacted in front of them. Each scene was labelled Danger Zone 1: Bedroom. Danger Zone 2: Kitchen. Danger Zone 3: Street. In each zone a fembly was being attacked by a membly. Then another scene flashed before her eyes. In this one small fembly and membly children were being attacked, sometimes by a fembly, sometimes by a membly.

Some observers wept and cried out. Others sat taking notes.

'This is the first learning schedule,' the Karkadile said. 'Here we come upon the source of evil in Thunderland. This is source 1. Later we will discover other sources. We will note them and observe them and deal with them.'

Its voice trailed off and Alice realised it was again asleep. While it slept, further scenes of cruelty were played out before her and in the end she put her hand before her eyes and cried out, 'Enough, enough.'

'Watch!' came the voice of the Karkadile. And Alice was transported high above the cliff over the valley of the war zone where below her the noise of battle continued. She thought she caught a glimpse of Bird's yellow feathers on the side of the hill. But she did not know if he was still writing his epics or if he too was part of the conflict they had tried to escape.

'This is source 2,' said the Karkadile. 'Beyond here is the Aspedilla who preys on the innocent; beyond it lie the feather-headed and the tear gatherers. All, all to a lesser or greater degree, are the sources. The source is unlimited. A sea without bottom. A well without end.

Who can change it? Only I, only I, the ageless Karkadilla can help them mend their ways.'

As it finished speaking there came a familiar blast of thunder. Flashes of lightning shot across the sky. Alice was propelled here and there, turned upside down, shaken inside out whilst beside her, imperturbable as ever was the Karkadile, sailing along on a wisp of cloud, oblivious to the hurricane they encountered.

Above the hubbub Alice managed to shout, 'I think the Voice is coming.'

She was right. Zooming across the lurid, lightning-spattered sky was the great mouth, complete with moustache and big teeth.

'Who dares?' Voice yelled. 'Who dares criticise? Who dares challenge? Who dares says no? Who dares question?'

'Take no notice,' said the Karkadile. 'Ignore it for long enough and it will go away.'

'I don't think so,' Alice said. 'I think it is here to stay.'

'So am I,' said the Karkadile. 'I have always been here. I always will be here. Windy weather won't shift me.'

'Whatever you do,' Alice shouted. 'Don't fall asleep.'

It was too late. It had already closed its eyes. With a triumphant leer, Voice opened its mighty teeth and snapped it up, leaving only the shell behind. In the shell was a shining pearl.

Alice snatched the pearl as she was tossed and tumbled and thrown from cloud to cloud and mountain top to mountain top.

'Oh Karkadile,' she cried. 'Why did you sleep, leaving only this pearl behind?'

She tumbled downwards towards the hill where she

had left Bird above the war zone. As she fell she heard his piping voice drifting up towards her, singing a lament for the Karkadile.

> *O Karkadile, why were you sleeping?*
> *O Karkadile, the world is weeping.*
> *Behold the light of noonday sun*
> *Has darkened as your life was done.*
> *Oh Karkadile, why did you leave us?*
> *There's no one left who will believe us.*
> *We'll haunt the night with our lament,*
> *Until you come to us again.*

'Until you, until you. No. Cross that out,' Alice heard Bird say as, fortunately for her sanity, she was whisked by the friendly storm out of earshot, still holding onto her pearl.

'Oh, Karkadile,' she whispered sadly. 'Why did you sleep?'

'Nonsense, my dear,' came the flutey voice straight from the pearl. 'Here I am again, merely in a different form. I am the pearl of great price. The seed of Wisdom.'

'I am sorry I missed your shell,' Alice said. 'It got carried away.'

'As we all do from time to time,' said the Karkadile. 'We must be vigilant at all times. Even when asleep. The Voice is now suffering from an enormous tummy-ache which will keep it silent for the time being. As for me, I must retreat for a while to refresh myself. A pearl of wisdom is all very well but it will not put the dinner on the table, now will it, eh? Direct me back home, if you please, and I will help you get on your way. I will not be able to sleep for ages. All this hoo-hahing and shouting is bad for the nerves if one had any, which fortunately, I do no.But I can always anticipate. Who knows when an unsympathetic nervous system may erupt?'

'Who knows, indeed,' thought Alice. 'I should like to be in Harmony Isle where there are certainties without rules, where there is peace without boredom, where there is pain which ends and joy which begins, where starshine and moonbeam soften the night, where rain quenches dust and life swings on a continuum of hope, where all things have their place, and all come to a due end.'

'You think good thoughts,' said the Karkadile. 'I would like you to collect a few to leave behind. I have a collection from other visitors which help me in my saddest moments when I have to visit the vale of tears.'

'What about the tear gatherer?' Alice asked. 'Where has she gone? And did she find the pool of tears?

But they were floating down over the green road, along the cliff, into the ruin, through the arched door and thankfully, back into the seashell where they were safe and sound with only the sea creatures floating by the window for distraction.

Chapter Ten

lice was relieved to be able to bring the Karkadile back safely. She expected the residents of the dome to show some surprise at its changed appearance but they carried on as if it was quite normal.

'Femblies,' the Karkadile pearl said, 'have great resilience. It is at once their safeguard and their downfall. They bear too much and survive too much. If they were frequently threatened with extinction their value would be higher. But the ability to adapt and change brings its own hazards. I now need time for new growth. Leave me here in the shade of the sea trees and follow your nose to the pool of tears where you will find your heart's desire.'

So saying, the pearl exuded a milky substance in which it lay suspended, awaiting, no doubt, some rebirth.

Alice would have liked a word of thanks but perhaps gratitude was not a virtue known in Thunderland.

How could she follow her nose? She might as well go anywhere. And so she did. She went anywhere, hither and thither, here and there, up and down until she came to the great door of exit. High, wide and handsome, it led to the outside world again. She knocked hard and had to force it open. Pushing and shoving, heaving and kicking, she burst out into the watery world that had surrounded her. Holding her nose with one hand and catching the fin of a passing sea-creature, she prayed for deliverance.

Her prayer was heard. She was borne upwards to the surface of the sea where a variety of creatures floundered, looking for directions.

'Which way?' some cried.

'This way,' others cried.

'No, no. This is the right way. That is the wrong way.'

And they all bumped into each other and issued instructions and gave directions and swam around in circles.

Alice joined a small group of femblies who seemed to be less agitated than the others. They lay on their backs, floating amiably, hands joined to form a circle so that they looked like a strange sea monster in the shape of a coloured wheel. As they floated they hummed in harmony. Alice swam around them for a while saying, 'Excuse me please, may I come in, may I join, excuse me please.' They ignored her until in exasperation she untwined two of the hands and slipped in. No one took any notice although Alice's large shape put the circle somewhat out of kilter. It sagged here and there, and flopped a bit until the group adjusted to her weight and size.

Eventually one of the group broke away and swam off, muttering about newcomers. Alice felt a little guilty but desperate needs take desperate deeds and she desperately needed someone to show her the way to the bay where her little boat might lie waiting for her. The group she had joined with their tranquil humming seemed at least sensible and although they may not have known where they were going they were reasonable and contented. Sooner or later, Alice reckoned, one would lead her where she wanted to go.

The sky darkened and suddenly the wheel collapsed. Everyone broke up and swam off. 'Don't tell me,' Alice thought, 'I just don't believe it. That Voice isn't coming back.'

She swam after one of the femblies, who seemed to be holding an object in her mouth. She looked purposeful, as if she knew where she was going.

Swimming up to her, Alice attempted a conversation, although it was somewhat difficult to talk and at the same time keep water from flowing into her mouth. This fembly was a very strong swimmer. Alice admired the way she was able to keep the object in her mouth while at the same time doing a breast stroke. The object was a vessel, a tear-shaped vessel. Alice was delighted to recognise the older fembly and her tear dish.

'I am pleased to see you again,' she cried out waterly. 'Where have you been?'

'I have been to see the Karkadile,' the older fembly said proudly. 'And I collected all the tears I needed.'

'I visited the Karkadile too but I didn't see you there,' Alice said.

'Why should you?' said the older fembly.

'We both went in different directions,' Alice said, remembering how she had branched off to visit the Aspedilla.

'You went in a different direction,' the older fembly said in a pained tone of voice. 'I went in the same direction but I got there just the same.'

'Where are the tears?' Alice asked. 'Your dish is empty.'

'I see you are still asking questions. What do you think you are swimming in?' the older fembly said. 'I got more than I bargained for. I looked for tears but I didn't expect this ocean. I think it covers the whole world. We will never get out of it.'

'We must just keep trying, 'Alice said bravely. 'We must just swim on.'

'Swim or sink,' the older fembly said grimly between her teeth, almost letting go of the tear dish.

'Perhaps I can help you,' Alice said. 'I could help you

carry the tear dish.'

'At last a sensible suggestion from the Harmony Isle interloper, the Miss Knowall who asked too many questions,' said the older fembly with rather a shade too much bitterness, Alice thought.

However, she let go the tear dish which Alice grasped between her teeth and they continued swimming, perhaps to the edge of the unknown world. By this time they were joined by a crowd of femblies and a large number of sea creatures. In the midst of all Alice spied the Aspedilla and a very ragged and crumpled Bird, his neck stretched as far as it would go, holding a piece of paper in his blue beak, valiantly trying to keep it dry.

The sky had lightened again. There was neither sight nor sound of the Voice although Alice had an uncanny sense of its presence hovering above them. Everyone surged forward. Stragglers to right and left moved into the group so that they progressed in a tightly packed mass with barely enough room to move their arms. Every now and again a swimmer changed strokes or lay on her back and floated for a while to relieve the stress.

After hours of effort Alice noticed a curve of sand ahead and beyond that a promontory. Around the corner, she was sure, was the bay and perhaps her boat.

She swam faster, hoping to outstrip the others. Sometimes she swallowed the salty tear water. Sometimes the tear dish filled and slopped over. Sometimes it turned upside down and she almost lost it.

She left the older fembly behind and could hear her crying, 'Bring back my tear dish. I need it.' She reached the very front of the mass of swimmers. Moving strongly ahead was a small determined figure. It was her friend, the first fembly she had met in Thunderland.

'Thank starshine I found you,' Alice gasped, forgetting about the tear dish and letting it float away. 'I thought I had lost you forever.'

The fembly did not answer but kept on swimming, muttering to herself, 'I must keep on. I must keep going. I must not give up.'

'If you relaxed a little,' Alice gasped, trying to keep pace with the little creature who was now zooming ahead, leaving a trail of spray behind her. 'You would last longer.'

'If I relax I will fizzle out,' the fembly said. 'There will be nothing left of me but my shell. Who will want an old shell? Nobody. No one wants a used-up shell of a fembly. Worn out at thirty-four, fat, fair and forty with gall bladder trouble, face creams and face lifts at fifty, wry and wrinkled at sixty. That's the future. What's it all about? What's the point? I found the windy ways of the world and there was nothing there for me. The ocean is full of tears. The Voice is everywhere. I've got to get away.'

'I found lovely places,' Alice said hopefully. 'I met the Karkadile.'

'Who cares?' said the little fembly fiercely, swimming so far ahead of Alice she could only just see her head bobbing above the waves.

Then there came the same old Thunder. Rocking and rolling across the sky. Singing a different song but with the same old menace.

> *I care for you my little pet.*
> *Don't leave me now or you'll get wet.*
> *This weary world has done me down.*
> *Love me and I'll be your circus clown.*
> *I'll make you live when you want to die.*
> *I'll make you laugh when you want to cry.*

Bass, Drums, Guitars. The tunes hit off the waves, following the fembly as she streaked like a typhoon across the horizon, whipping up the waves as she went. The last Alice saw of her she was still going strong but so was Thunder Voice with his vast array of musical instruments.

Alice rounded the promontory corner and saw the cove where she had landed. She swam strongly towards it putting as great a distance as she could between herself and the crowd. She heard Bird piping some deathly ditty about the strength of his wing and his loneliness and his mother who did not love him and his father who died too soon after the long walks they took in the meadows of youth and the long-haired grasses of maiden plants and their luscious fruits and how he was a poet who loved all femblies. And Alice with heartfelt conviction echoed the femblies' cry, 'Who Cares?' as she swam gratefully into the shelter of the cove.

Here was clear blue water. Her feet touched the bottom and she half-swam, half-walked the last few yards to the shore. She had no time to spare. She stumbled towards the outcrop of rock where she expected to find her boat. It was there, safe and sound. She climbed into it and then leaped back in horror as she felt a sharp little claw clutching her ankle. A small voice like the cry of a kitten mewed, 'Help me, help me.' Lying at the bottom of the boat was the mamba who had climbed up her shoulder and run away on the first days of her visit to Thunderland.

'You cratureen,' said Alice pityingly. 'You are in a state. What happened you at all?'

'You may well ask,' said the mamba. 'All all happened. Too much to tell. I have drunk from the well of plenty and I am almost poisoned. No one can cure me. I tried to find the Karkadile but she was otherwise engaged.'

'Yes,' said Alice. 'She was with me.'

'Then,' said the mamba gravely 'You have been the death of me.'

'Surely it was the well of plenty that was the death of you.'

'Cause and effect. Search the cause, you will find the effect. You are the cause, this the effect.'

'I cannot agree,' Alice said. 'However we have no time for debate. I had better get help for you.'

With a heavy heart she went to the shoreline, took off her shirt and began to wave it wildly, calling, 'Help, Help,' at the same time in the direction of the swimming mass.

It did not take long for the whole dripping mass to arrive on her beach. They shook themselves free of water, ran around to dry themselves, chirped and chattered and grumbled and ignored her cries for help for the mamba until she stood on the rock and yelled as loudly as she could for a full minute.

Bird heard her first. He fluttered up to her, his broken wing drooping, his poems tied around his neck. Then the older fembly came, with her tear dish, Alice was glad to see. Then the Aspedilla and finally the multifarious femblies. They stared at the mamba lying so pale and still at the bottom of the boat.

The older fembly said, 'It has the too much sickness. It will have to do with too little for a long time if it is to recover.'

'Too much of what? Alice asked. But no one saw fit to answer her. They busied themselves gathering bits of flotsam and pieces of jetsam along the shore. The older fembly took the mamba out of the boat and walked up and down cradling it and crooning to it. Bird sharpened his quill on a stone. The Aspedilla took out a handkerchief and shook a bunch of red berries out. A small fembly came forward and offered to crush the berries to make a drink for the mamba. Others began to gather timber for a fire. A group walked along the water's edge, staring at the sky and forecasting weathers. Another group began to talk about electing a leader. The Aspedilla tried to look modest but made sure he was seen at the front of the group. When Bird heard the talk he began to recite one of his poems, saying that of course he was not putting himself forward but he knew that they knew that he had all the qualities of leadership the position required and that without boasting he could say that he was the best creature for the job. He would lead them off this desert island into a wonderful future.

Alice called out, 'This is not a a desert island. This is only a peninsula. It belongs to the rest of the land. It is part of it.'

But they were too busy electing a leader to listen to her.

'What will the leader do?' Alice cried. 'Where will it lead? I have asked two questions. Where are you, Voice?'

For she reckoned that a blast or two of Thunder might straighten out their heads. But there was no Voice. It had gone over the high hills and the high winds to nowhere.

While all the discussing and arguing was going on, Alice pulled the boat down to the shore. No one cared. She pushed it onto the water, sat inside it. Still no one cared. She took the oars and rowed slowly away.

Every now and again she looked back towards the group on the sand. Overhead, clouds gathered. A few raindrops splashed onto her face. She rowed faster. It grew darker. In a little while Thunderland was covered in mist. She could not see the shoreline or the rocky promontory, or the high cliff where she had found the Karkadile. To the west was a glimmer of the setting sun. It sent golden rays in long bright ribs of light across the waters. Somewhere ahead of her the fembly was swimming bravely away. Alice rowed towards her, knowing that sooner or later she would catch up to her. Sooner or later the fembly would make her way, with or without Alice, to the wonderful land of Harmony Isle. But one thing was sure, thought Alice. 'I'll be there to greet her.'